Wounded

Wounded

Ben Burgess Jr.

URBAN
Renaissance

www.urbanbooks.net

Urban Books, LLC
300 Farmingdale Road, NY-Route 109
Farmingdale, NY 11735

ISBN 13: 978-1-64556-135-4
ISBN 10: 1-64556-135-6

First Mass Market Printing December 2020
First Trade Paperback Printing December 2019
Printed in the United States of America

10 9 8 7 6 5 4 3 2 1

Distributed by Kensington Publishing Corp.
Submit Orders to:
Customer Service
400 Hahn Road
Westminster, MD 21157-4627
Phone: 1-800-733-3000
Fax: 1-800-659-2436

Dedicated to my friends:

Christine Hazel
Dishea Paschall
CJ Mottershead
Kelly Sanchez
Antonia Cato
Christiana Harrell
Jill Carroll
Nicole Talleur
Katie Piccolo

I wrote this book in honor of my friends who are a part of the LGBT community. While I am not a part of the community, I thank all of you for showing me that love is love and no one should be judged for who they are or who they love.

*"You can accept or reject the way you are treated by other people, but until you heal the **wounds** of your past, you will continue to bleed."*

—Iyanla Vanzant

One

Shock and Awe

"Oh my God! I can't believe I . . . we . . . just did that," she said.

I smiled as I lay comfortably in my bed with my hands behind my head. I watched this woman, whom I met at the bar, frantically gather her clothes that were sprawled all over the beige carpet. With the pile by her feet, she sat down on the bed and shook her head in disbelief. She frantically searched through the pile for her panties and quickly put them on. I enjoyed seeing that look on her face—the look of confusion and shame. No matter how much she tried to deny it, or how hard she tried to hide it in the deepest, darkest corner of her mind, she got fucked by a woman—and she *loved* it! She quickly tried to put on her clothes while avoiding eye contact with me.

"This never happened; I'm a married woman," she said.

I smiled at her. "Sure. Whatever you say."

"No, seriously, this didn't happen. I'm not a lesbian. I . . . I don't know what came over me."

I knew her type. I had dealt with them hundreds of times before. She would go home to her husband and pretend like nothing happened, but our intimacy had unleashed something in her. Bombarded with thoughts and questions, she would remember every lick and touch I gave her. Her mind would frequently drift to the memory of our sexual connection. She would realize the feelings of elation and the intensity of the orgasms she experienced with me had trumped anything she'd ever felt with a man. Before she knew it, she would be yet another woman who I reformed. It was inevitable. No man could ever know a woman's body like a woman, and there was nothing they could offer that a woman couldn't, except for being able to provide sperm to procreate.

I loved converting breeders! There were the rare occasions when some of them became pillow princesses or closet cases, but it didn't matter. That door had been unlocked, and they would eventually want to experience that ecstasy with a woman again. While I'm a hunter for alleged "straight" women, I'm no monster. I only go after the ones who make my "gaydar" go off. If I have the slightest sense they have an attraction to women, I go after them.

I was born gay. I've known it since I was a child, but some of us try to suppress what we truly desire and need to be awaken.

I met this woman hanging out at the Cubbyhole in Manhattan. Her friends knew what was up. None of them tried to interfere or stop her from leaving with me. She was hanging out at a bar for lesbians and ended up leaving with one. She wasn't too drunk or high. I made sure the choice was her volition. Once she came to my apartment located in Co-op City, Bronx, it was a wrap.

She continued to get dressed and hastily left my apartment. There was no love lost or sadness on my part. It was all just a game to me. With these green eyes, pretty face, and voluptuous figure, I had no problem attracting other lesbians. The real challenge was bedding so-called straights. Opening their eyes to a new world and awakening them to a realm that isn't dominated by men is the greatest gift I can give another woman.

I rolled over in my bed and drifted off to sleep, smiling over my latest conquest. She'd be back.

They always come back.

I tossed and turned in my sleep. Visions of my childhood haunted my dreams. Every night, I'm plagued by recurring nightmares. I felt the hands of those dirty men reaching for me, touching and groping me. My dreams took me back to that abandoned truck in Hunts Point in the Bronx—those horrible memories that started when I was 10 years old.

"So, you got that for me?" my mother, Joan, asked.

"I said I did, right? You gonna let me get that?" the strange man asked, pointing at me. He stared at me. His eyes were as dark as marbles. He smiled, revealing a row of gold teeth. I would never forget his smile. Those gold teeth would haunt me forever.

I looked at my mother to see her reaction. She was fidgeting. She hastily rubbed the sides of her arms. She wore a face of uncertainty and desperation. I had seen her like this countless times. My mother was feenin'.

"Uh . . . okay . . . yeah, but . . . Just take it easy on her, okay? She's my kid."

I didn't know what she meant by that statement . . . until I felt his hands touch my chest. I cringed and ran behind my mother.

"Don't worry. I'm not gonna hurt her. I'm gonna take good care of her," he laughed.

"Now, Samantha . . . This is Mommy's friend. He just wants to play with you a little bit. He's not going to hurt you."

"Mommy, please don't leave me with him."

There was a look of fear and desperation on her face. "Calm down, Sammy. Everything is OK," she said, patting my hand.

"Yo, we doin' this shit or what?" he asked. He grabbed his crotch and looked impatient.

"Yeah, give me a minute," Joan said. She knelt in front of me and wrapped her arms around me.

"Sammy, do what he tells you, okay? Don't fight with him and don't talk back. He's not going to hurt you . . . I promise."

"Please, Mommy, I don't want to go with him," I pleaded.

She put her finger to my lips, silencing my protest. "It's okay . . . It's okay. Everything is going to be fine." My mother turned back to the man.

"Okay, daddy, she's ready. I'm jonesing real bad. I need it."

The man laughed in her face. "Nah, I don't know if I want to give it to you now. You took too long," he laughed, waving a small, clear baggie containing tan powder.

"Come on, daddy, don't be like that. I got her here for you like I promised."

"Well, now, I want more. Come here and bless me first; then I'll take her."

He unzipped his pants and pulled out his penis.

My mother didn't hesitate. She knelt in the dirt next to the abandoned U-Haul truck and took him in her mouth. With his head tilted back, he gripped the top of her head, using it as leverage as he attempted to gag her with his penis. I watched my mother's head bob as she eagerly tried to please him. He stopped her.

"All right, bring her over here," he instructed.

My mother wiped her mouth with the back of her hand; then she kissed my forehead. "Okay, be a good girl, Sammy. Do everything he tells you. Don't fight with him and try not to cry."

"What do you mean by that, Mommy?"

She pulled me toward him by my right arm. I dropped to the ground, trying my hardest to fight going to him. She dragged me, leaving me at his feet. He flicked the plastic baggie he had been holding at her forehead. It bounced off and fell to the ground. She quickly crawled on her knees, snatched it up, reached in the right pocket of her ripped blue jeans, and pulled out a lighter and hypodermic needle.

"All right, little momma, you're coming with me," the man said.

I kicked and scratched, fighting to keep him away from me.

"I like when they're feisty," he laughed, picking me up. He threw me on a mattress in the abandoned truck.

I continued to kick and scream as he crept toward me. I kicked him in his face with all my strength. Blood dripped from his nose and mouth. That pissed him off. He slapped the shit out of me, inflicting the same damage on me. The blow was so hard that it left me dizzy. Even though I was disoriented, I screamed. I cried. I felt my clothes being ripped off me. I saw my mother a few feet away. I reached out for her.

"Mommy, please! Help me!" I screamed, but my pleas fell on deaf ears.

Her eyes widened and turned glassy. Her head dipped, and her body relaxed. She couldn't hear my screams. She couldn't help me. My mother was gone, lost in that magical world of heroin. The man ripped off my Hello Kitty panties. His filthy left hand covered my mouth. I heard the clank of his belt as his pants fell around his ankles. I felt his penis searching for the entrance of my vagina. My cries only excited him more as he applied his full body weight on top of me and had his way with me.

I gasped and woke up screaming and trembling. Dreams of the countless times I had experienced situations like that as a child haunted me daily. It took me a few minutes to realize that I wasn't in that horrific day, and I wasn't that scared little girl anymore. I lay in my bed, crying and rocking in the fetal position. Quickly, I grabbed my pack of Marlboro cigarettes off my nightstand and lit one, taking long, quick drags to calm myself down. I stretched my arms above my head, then rolled over on my side to look at the time on my alarm clock; it was two in the afternoon. I shook off that terrible dream, got up, showered, and began my day.

I don't have a family. The only people who I am remotely close to, I guess what you would call my "family," are my best friends, Silka and Jaime. I've been tight with them since our days in foster care. We've been through countless foster homes and homeless shelters together; we've run away from those same places together. After numerous times of being reunited in those hellholes, we took it as destiny telling us that we were meant to be in one another's lives. We've cried together, supported each other, and I would die for them.

I called Silka to see if she would be down with going to the gym with me.

"What's up, sis? What are you doing right now?" I asked.

"Nothing. Enjoying being off from teaching those little bastards today."

Silka's real name was Jackie. A Spanish teacher at John Philip Sousa Junior High in the Bronx, she was the mature one of the group. She was married but still had that feisty, flirtatious nature I loved. Jaime and I credited those traits to her African American and Latino bloodlines.

"You feel like rolling with me to the gym?" I asked.

"Chick, you don't even go to my gym. The only reason why you're even asking me is so you can try to bed that receptionist, Crystal."

I giggled. "Listen here, breeder. We all know you wish you had my lifestyle. Dominic is just a front."

I heard her cracking up on the other end.

"You have no sense; you know that? Don't you have to work at the club tonight? Aren't you going to be tired later if you work out before you dance?"

"Hell nah! It doesn't take that much energy to shake my ass in front of those clowns and take their money."

My main job headlining as a stripper at J's Gentlemen's Quarters on 233rd Street provided me with the bulk of my money while I worked on building my side hustle photography business, which I ran out of my apartment for the time being. Having a lengthy criminal record limited my ability to find better jobs, so I did what I could to get by. Even though I made a killing stripping, I knew that window of opportunity was short, and the money from that would sooner or later dry up. Eventually, I wanted to stop stripping and focus exclusively on my photography business, although I had no idea when that would come to fruition. My photography started as a hobby. At first, I used it as a gimmick to get girls to pose practically nude in my apartment, so I could fuck them, but I started to really take a liking to it. I took a few classes and got nice with it. I do take it seriously and want to make a career out of it, but I still use it as one of the main tools to persuade women to come to my place so I could bed them. Crystal was next on my fuck-it list!

"All right, pick me up in fifteen minutes. Dominic took off from work too. I'll have him watch Georgia while we go work out," Silka said.

"Cool, let me get myself together, and I'll see you in a few."

We said our goodbyes, and I ended the call.

Although I hated men and would never admit it openly, Dom was cool people. A muscular Italian guy with dark brown eyes and hair, he was a New York City firefighter for Ladder 39. Silka had a small kitchen fire in the apartment she shared with Jaime during the time I was serving time in Albion Correctional Facility, upstate, after getting busted for prostitution. Dom responded to the call. To hear Silka tell the story, it was love at first sight. She married him shortly after I got out so I could be in the wedding.

I looked for faults in him, but he treated Silka like a queen. Still, I kept a close eye on him. Even though he was a decent guy, I always gave him a shitty attitude, provoking him to snap so his true colors would show. I haven't met a man yet that hasn't fucked a woman over in some capacity. I can't lie. A part of me was envious of her family life. While I could never have a relationship with a man—ugh, the thought alone makes me queasy—I would like to have a daughter one day like Silka has. I honestly would enjoy raising a kid and having the chance to correct all the things that were fucked up with my childhood.

I finished getting ready and put on some skintight black leggings with a matching top and headed to pick Silka up in my Jeep Cherokee SRT8. When I pulled in front of her house and honked, Dom came out holding the baby. He knocked on my window. I rolled my eyes as I reluctantly rolled it down. He leaned his head in my car window and said, "Hey, Sam!"

"Dom . . ."

"Silka should be out any minute."

I rolled my eyes at him. "You mean she isn't going to leave me out here all day? God bless her."

He ignored my sarcasm and changed the subject. "So . . . What's on the agenda for the two of you today?"

"None of your business, man; damn," I sighed. "God, where is she so you can stop fucking talking to me?" I asked, pretending to look around to annoy him.

He laughed at my rudeness. "All right . . . I'll leave you alone. It's time to feed the baby anyway. Make sure you take care of my wife."

As I waved him away, Silka walked out of the house and kissed him. I looked away disgusted as they did their usual lovey-dovey bullshit.

"Am I still your least favorite white boy?" he asked, smiling at me.

"Dom, if you don't get away from my ride, I'm going to fuck you up."

He laughed. "I love you too, Sam."

"Ain't shit funny over here, white boy."

"Sam, please try to be nice to my husband," Silka said calmly.

"I always try, but I don't always succeed." We chuckled as she got in.

Silka was used to my bitchy attitude toward Dom. I think the reason she didn't get upset about it was the fact she knew I cared for her. She understood it was my twisted way of trying to protect her. Growing up together, she loved me for who I was—quirks and all.

Silka looked fine dressed in her red, seamless sports bra and black, form-fitting leggings. She had a body on her. She was a shapely five foot two with a hearty ass, gorgeous caramel skin, and full D-cup breasts. If I didn't look at her as a sister, she would definitely be the type I would love to turn out.

"Girl, your Jeep is too damn loud. I heard this shit coming a mile away," Silka said jokingly.

"What can I say? I like powerful things."

"Powerful? This shit sounds like a damn tank coming down the block."

I smirked. "Hey, now . . . Keep talking about my shit, and I'll make your ass walk to the gym."

"Did you forget you're coming to the gym as *my* guest? You better come correct when you talk to *this* queen."

I loved our closeness.

We walked into Bally's on Bartow Avenue. I immediately spotted Crystal at the front desk. She smiled when she saw me. I'd been working on this girl for a couple of months now. I didn't have a membership and had no desire to get one, but I'd continue to pay the guest fee until I beat that. I waved at her. Silka looked at me, laughed, and shook her head.

"All right, playa, handle your business. I'm going to warm up on the step machine. Meet me over there after you finish courting your ghetto princess."

As soon as Silka stepped away, Crystal approached me.

"Hey, there!" she said.

"How are you doing, shorty? You're looking as sexy as ever."

She blushed. I knew she was feeling me, but I was getting impatient. I wanted to hit that, and I wanted it *now*. My gaydar screamed whenever I saw her. She was overly touchy with me, and besides flirting, I always caught her staring at me. I sensed deep down she was gay; she just needed the right woman to bring it out of her. Crystal was five foot four with shapely hips and modest C-cup breasts. She had thick lips that were accentuated with the bright red lipstick she always wore.

"I'm good. When are you going to get a membership here so you can visit me more often?"

Her nonstop flirting was turning me on. I kept promoting my photography business to draw her to my condo.

I licked my lips and replied, "I'll get a membership today if you stop by my place after work and let me photograph you."

She hesitated. "Uh . . . I . . . I don't know. I'm dressed like a bum today. I'm not even wearing anything decent enough to be photographed in."

"Chill, shorty. I'll take you shopping for a few outfits after you get off. The outfits are on me. So, what's up?"

A huge smile came across her face. "A'ight, cool. I get off at five."

I knew that. I did my research and had her schedule memorized already.

"Okay, cool. I can't wait," I said.

I went to the locker room, put my gym bag in a locker, and headed toward Silka on the cardio machines.

"I'm going to turn her out today. I know it," I said.

Silka laughed and shook her head. "You're crazy. That poor girl doesn't know what she's getting herself into."

"You got that right. I'm going to wear her out!"

"I'll call Dom to pick me up when we're done here so you can focus on your future conquest."

"See, this is why you're my sister!"

Silka laughed and shook her head again.

We trained our legs thoroughly, doing lunges, glute bridges, and squats until we felt like we would puke. Being the headliner at a strip club, I had to be disciplined with my body. If I didn't maintain a good diet along with keeping my ass and tits firm and perky, some other heifer would come on the scene and mess up my cash flow. My window in that business was short, so I stashed as much loot as I could to get this photography shit started.

We finished our workout. Dom picked up Silka, and I stuck my tongue out at her as she waved.

When Crystal got off work, I took her to the Westchester Mall in White Plains. If dropping wads of cash would get me some of that ass, I'd spend whatever was necessary. I bought her some cute outfits from Express and Victoria's Secret. She modeled the sexy lingerie for me in the dressing room. I couldn't wait to get her back to my apartment so that I could charm her out of them.

On the drive to my place, I filled her head with compliments while my thoughts were on seeing her spread eagle on my bed.

"You looked so hot in that lingerie you had on," I said.

"You really think so?"

"Baby girl, as a woman who wears lingerie regularly for a living, trust me when I tell you, your body in those outfits could put a lot of these whack-ass strippers I work with to shame."

"Thank you!"

"No need to thank me; it's the truth."

It was partially true. There were some broads I worked with that I'd say her body was better than.

The look on her face let me know my seduction was working. I opened the door and let her walk in first.

"You can use my bedroom to get changed."

"All right. Thanks for this."

"Nah, thank you."

I set my lights, background, and camera, but I didn't plan on taking too many pictures. As soon as I saw my opening, I'd act on it and turn her ass out! The first outfit she had on was a nice business suit. I snapped a few photos and then told her to put on the lingerie. She came out looking exquisite. She had on a black bustier with matching black lace French-cut panties and stockings.

The outfit hugged her petite shape. This was my opportunity.

"Damn, ma, you look good as hell."

"Thank you," she blushed.

"Hold up. You got something on your face."

There wasn't shit on her face. I only said that to get close to her. She wiped at her face.

"Did I get it?" she asked.

"Nah, I'll get it. Come here."

She walked up to me. While cradling her face in my hands, I kissed her softly on the lips. The kiss caught her off guard at first, and it seemed like she was thinking of pulling away, but she relaxed in my hands. She was mine. Her eyes were closed as if she were savoring the moment. I pulled her closer to me and kissed her over and over. My hands wandered over her body. Soft moans escaped her mouth as she became lost in my embrace.

Suddenly, she opened her eyes.

"Damn, I swear you're a man in a beautiful woman's body."

"Baby girl, I'm *better* than a man."

"I'm not gay, though."

"Shhh. Don't worry about labels. Just enjoy the moment."

"I'm really not, though. I have a man and—"

I stopped her bantering by continuously kissing her. My gaze never left hers as I took my time and slowly pulled her panties down. I laid her down, caressing her thigh with my left hand while I rubbed the head of her clitoris with my right. My mouth went to her ample breasts.

Her heart was pounding. Her breathing was choppy. I positioned myself between her legs.

"Wait. I'm really not gay. This is too much."

"Just relax, ma, and enjoy this. Let me please you," I whispered.

A tranquil expression was on her face. The gentle way I spoke soothed her. I flicked my tongue on her pearl, switching up the sensation of long, broad licks to circles. I tenderly sucked on each of her lips before massaging the inside of her vagina with my fingers.

"Oh my God . . . Oooh!"

I raised my mouth off her but continued to use my fingers as I asked her questions. "How does that feel? Do you like that, baby?"

"Shit shit shit . . . I'm gonna fucking come!"

I loved pleasing women. Their pleasure gave me pleasure. Having sex with a woman who is new to this experience gave me a feeling of control and completeness.

Crystal grabbed my long, curly hair and held my face in her love as she came intensely. Then she took off her bra. I took off my clothes and lay down on top of her. Our bodies pressed tightly together. Our legs overlapped as I ground my thigh into her sweetness. I simultaneously massaged mine on hers.

"Shit, this feels so fucking good," Crystal yelled out.

"I want to please you. I want you to enjoy this," I whispered in her ear.

I reveled at the sight of her, lost in pleasure from my gentle kisses and sucks on her neck. I let my hands slide down her body, skillfully inserting my middle finger into her. I massaged her clit with my thumb. Her back arched.

She cursed repeatedly. I inserted a second finger and thrust them in and out of her love. I fucked her, giving her mind-blowing orgasms until she couldn't take any more.

When it was over, she took a long shower and got dressed in my bathroom. She came out of the bathroom with her head down and avoided eye contact with me. She looked exhausted and ashamed; I had a smirk on my face.

"You good, ma? I should have your portraits ready for you sometime next week."

She gave me a curt smile. "Thanks, but let's address the massive elephant in the room. I've never done . . . this . . . before."

"Done what? What do you mean?" I knew exactly what she meant, but I enjoyed seeing the discomfort and confusion on her face. I wanted to hear her say it and admit that she got fucked properly by a woman.

"I've never been with a woman before. I don't know what any of this means. Am I gay, bi, or straight? I don't know what to think anymore."

Tears began to form in her eyes at her confusion.

"Well, shorty, it seems like you need to do some soul searching. I know what I am, but you need to figure out what you are."

Since she didn't have a car and usually took the bus to work, I decided to do her a favor and drive her to her apartment that she shared with her man. The car ride was quiet. She only spoke to provide me with her address for the GPS. When I got to her place, she quickly reached for the door handle, but I gently tugged on her arm, pulled her to me, and kissed her on the lips. Again, she didn't resist. She exited my car with a confused look and headed off to a false haven with her man.

I headed back to my place to get ready for work at the club. I reflected on what I had done. I would never go back to that gym with Silka again. Luckily for me, Crystal and I didn't waste time working on a membership for me. Unless she called me, I'd probably never fuck with her again. I had accomplished what I set out to do. My mission was complete. I didn't care if I left her questioning her sexuality. Today got her sprung. I helped to awaken another lesbian into the world, enjoyed myself while doing it, and I felt pretty damn good about myself. Deep down, I wanted a woman who I could truly share myself with. I wanted an emotional connection beyond the physical bullshit, but until I found her, I'd continue to enjoy turning bitches out.

Two

Almighty Isis

The lights were lowered. The music stopped. The crowd went wild because they knew what was coming. I peeked out of the curtain; then I stretched, bending over and clutching the back of my calves to loosen up before I hit the stage. The bouncers wore their usual tight black shirts with *Security* embroidered on the back and scanned the crowd. The club was packed tonight. Seeing me, the DJ gave me a wink and a nod.

"Everybody, get ready to unload your pockets. Here she comes, the queen of J's Gentlemen's Quarters. The one . . . the only . . . the Almighty Isis!"

All eyes were on me as I stood on stage wearing only a black G-string, gyrating and shaking my ass seductively to Rhianna's "Where Have You Been?" The spotlights felt like heat lamps. My six-inch, black Jimmy Choo stiletto heels, and long, toned legs only added to my Amazonian, five-foot-eight, full-figured frame.

The music boomed from the huge speakers on the walls. The crowd cheered; they all wanted me. I felt them fucking me with their eyes. I felt the wind whisking by me as they reached for me. I winked and blew kisses, smirking at the sight of them throwing their hard-earned money on the stage. All types of people came through the club's doors—businessmen, athletes, drug dealers, pimps, and thugs—but they were all chumps to me. I'd watched these losers remove their wedding rings and call their significant others to lie about their whereabouts. I'm sure a majority of them had families or kids that could use the extra dollars, but they would rather spend it here. So, I gladly took these suckers' money.

I always loved attention. Dancing seductively on stage and taking my clothes off felt like second nature to me. As a child, I was groped and forced to do so many disgusting and horrible acts that dancing with my clothes off as a profession felt natural.

I finished my routine and seductively gathered the rest of the money that was thrown and scattered across the hardwood stage by my feet. I sashayed off the stage and headed to the curtains when some dark-skinned, bucktoothed brother with braids wearing an expensive pin-striped suit tugged on my leg. I frowned and pulled away.

"Don't fucking grab on me," I yelled.

"Excuse me. I don't mean to push up on you, but my employer, Mr. Smith, would like to pay you two grand if you would grace him and his wife with your presence in the VIP room. Can they pay to play?"

Some of the bouncers came over, but I waved them off. He wasn't dressed like a slouch, so I was interested in hearing more of what the bucktoothed brother had to say.

While some people paid for risqué lap dances in the champagne rooms, those with *real* money who wanted more, paid extra to go into the VIP rooms. Once you were in those rooms, whatever happened behind those doors stayed behind those doors, and anything was fair game. At the strip club, you could make decent money shaking your ass, but if you wanted to make more significant money, for the right price, it paid to sell your ass in the VIP rooms.

He pointed toward a white couple. They looked like they had money. The man looked like he was in his mid-forties—clean-cut, graying brown hair, and a medium build. He was wearing a shiny gold Rolex on his wrist, and his clothes screamed of wealth. At least that gave me confidence that he wasn't full of shit. The woman was attractive, with blond hair, blue eyes, and big tits. Mr. Smith was most likely a fake name. These types never used their real names around here. I had done shit like this countless times for less. Two Gs was good money. I wasn't turning that shit down. Most of the time, couples that were well off came so that the men could watch me fuck their wives. It was common for their women to try to play it off. They would claim it's nothing serious and that they had a little fetish for it or it was something they toyed with in college that they wanted to experience again. I knew the truth: they were gay and wanted to get fucked in a way their husbands couldn't provide.

"Cool. I'm in. Tell them I'll meet them there in ten minutes and they better not be playing with my money."

A huge grin was on his face. The stupid lackey was happy to report to his boss that I was down for the cause. I laughed to myself. White people in this neighborhood were always sketchy. Usually, they were cops looking for drugs or just needing their chocolate fix.

As I made my way through the crowd, men tried to grab my hand, pinch my ass, and grope my tits. The moment some of these men tried to get too touchy and reached for my goodies, the bouncers were right there to keep them in check. The bouncers were quick to remind them of the club's strict "no touching policy," and they loved to enforce it and make examples of people by beating the shit out them and kicking them out.

I walked over to my girl, Jaime, who was bartending.

"Sis, hook me up with two shots of Hennessey," I said.

Jaime was dressed to get lots of tips. She had on a white V-neck top—without a bra—that showcased her cleavage and hardened nipples. She wore tight black yoga pants that clung to her round ass.

"Uh-oh, I know something is going down if you're asking for shots this early into your shift. Sam, what are you up to?"

I smirked. She knew exactly what the look on my face meant.

"You really need to stop fucking with people like that. It's going to come back and bite you in the ass one day. Do you want to get picked up by the cops and do time again?" she said while pouring my shots.

"I can't turn down two grand. Your ass needs to get into this too."

"Girl, please, I could never do that. You need to be careful, Sammy," she told me. Jaime knew there was no way to deter me from my decision.

I winked at her and downed my shots. I needed the liquid courage to help with not feeling sick to my stomach if "Mr. Smith" tried to touch me. I knew he would want to put his grubby hands on me, so numbing myself as fast as possible was a must. Most of these white guys got off and felt powerful by fucking black women.

After that, I went to the dressing room. There were a handful of girls in there, and they all ignored my presence. Some were crowded in front of mirrors piling makeup on their ugly-ass faces while some were using flat irons to fix their fucked-up long weaves and touching up the polish on their fake airbrushed nails. There were a few that were prancing around in their heels practicing their routines, but I didn't give a shit about the other dancers and vice versa. They were too busy getting ready for their own sets to acknowledge me while I freshened up. I wiped myself down with baby wipes, spritzed some perfume on myself, and adjusted my cleavage, tightening the straps on my bra to give my tits a little extra oomph and make my boobs appear bigger. I gave myself a once-over, placed my earnings from earlier in my locker, grabbed my wristlet, checked to make sure I had condoms and lube, and headed to their room.

Despite Jerrod, the club owner, being a cheap bastard, he actually spent a decent amount of money to make the VIP rooms look on point. They were sectioned off into nice soundproof rooms. Usually, there would be a bouncer posted to stand guard by the door of each VIP room whenever they were occupied to protect the strippers, but unless we had a bad feeling and didn't trust the clients, we usually told the bouncers to take a hike.

"All right, big man, you can take an extended cigarette break. I'll be fine," I said to the huge bouncer.

He had to be about six foot ten with arms bigger than my legs, and his T-shirt looked painted on him.

"You sure, Isis? There are two guys and a woman in there," he said, looking concerned.

"I don't want to add to your spank bank, but this wouldn't be the first time I took on that type of a combination. I'll be all right. You can go."

He smiled, laughed, and walked away.

When I walked inside the room, the bucktoothed brother was standing by the door while Mr. Smith and the woman were sitting on the black leather sofa.

"Hey! Nice of you to join us," Mr. Smith said.

"What's your name, darling?" the white woman asked. I assumed she was his wife.

"Isis," I responded.

"Not your stage name, darling. What's your *real* name?"

"Isis. What are your real names?" I fired back.

Mr. Smith laughed.

"My name is Virginia—" she managed to get out before her husband interrupted her.

"We're the Smiths," he answered, then frowned at his wife.

"Exactly . . . That's what I thought. Look, I'm not up for games, and you are asking way too many questions, white lady. What are you, five-o or something?"

Virginia looked confused. "Five-o?" she asked, staring at the bucktoothed brother that came with them.

"She asking if you two are cops," he explained.

She laughed off the accusation of her and her husband being undercovers. I, on the other hand, didn't find shit funny.

"You're laughing, but you still didn't answer my question. Are you guys cops?"

"If it will put your mind at ease to hear me say it, no, we are not cops," Virginia said.

"Do you have my money? I'm not about wasting my time, so if we're going to 'play,' I want my money up front, in cash."

"All right, all right. I respect that. A young woman who is about business . . . I like that," Mr. Smith said.

The bucktoothed brother handed me a black plastic bag and then excused himself from the room. Inside the bag was an envelope packed with a stack of hundreds. The money was already wrapped in a small wad. I quickly counted the money to make sure it was all there, and then I separated the majority of the money because I knew the club owner, Jerrod, would want his cut at some point when he saw me later tonight. After putting the money in my small Prada wristlet wallet, I faced the Smiths.

"Again, are you guys cops?" I asked bluntly.

Virginia laughed. "No, my dear. Do we look like cops?"

"That sound exactly like something a cop would say."

"I assure you, we are *not* cops, but since we're being so frank, the reason why I am here is that I want to get fucked by a woman," she said.

I turned to Mr. Smith. "Are you joining in too?"

"Afterward. I'll let her have her fun and watch you two play first; then I would like to have you to myself."

Virginia removed her clothes. I took off mine. I headed over to her and firmly grabbed her ass with both hands. She kissed me hungrily. I felt her energy. Her body was telling me that she needed this fuck. I pushed her down on the red leather couch. She licked her lips and spread her legs. She was eager for me. I kissed her, tracing the inside of her thighs with my fingers. I licked her neck, slowly making a trail with my tongue to her belly button and then to her thighs. Her pussy was so unbelievably wet. I saw the moisture coating her inner thighs.

She smelled very good, which was a plus. I licked the inside of her thighs. Her body shivered. I sucked on her pussy lips individually and then licked the middle of her flower. My eyes fixated on her face to gauge her response. I watched as she moaned and massaged her breasts while I feasted on her. Her hands gripped the top of my head.

"Fuck me," she demanded.

When she said that, I quickly inserted two fingers inside her and used my thick, full lips to suck on the head of her clitoris. I massaged the top of her vagina, using my fingertips in varied motions. She screamed out all types of curses, while I pressed my face deeper into her treasure. I increased the pace of my massage. Her moans of ecstasy bounced off the walls in the room. Her juices flowed like a river, saturating my long, manicured fingers. I slid a third finger inside of her, and her body went into sensory overload. She writhed wildly. I loved it. Her body was under my control, and there was nothing she could do about it. I enjoyed having her husband there to see it. I wanted him to understand firsthand that nothing he had between his legs would ever equate to the power I possessed. When she came, the uncontrollable spasm of her vagina muscles on my fingers turned me on.

"Oh . . . Jesus!" she shouted. Her body bucked out of control.

I wiped my face and smiled. Mr. Smith kissed Virginia's forehead as she twitched and jerked on the couch.

"Are you happy, honey?" he asked, caressing her face lovingly.

"Very!" she said with a naughty smile.

Virginia was still twitching from the aftershock of coming powerfully. She looked exhausted and satisfied lying on the couch. Mr. Smith picked up her clothes and handed them to her. He clapped his hands, rubbed them together, and said, "All right, honey, it's my turn to have fun now. Take a walk."

Virginia stopped smiling. She appeared irritated but did as she was told, got dressed, and left the room. As soon as the door closed, Mr. Smith's entire attitude changed. He had a cold demeanor and seemed angry. His eyes blackened. They looked as if they were darkened with malice by the painful truth that his wife was a dyke.

"All right, bitch, on your knees."

I dropped down to my knees and came face-to-face with his dick. I put the tip of it in my mouth and deep throated him, sucking him swiftly. He held my face. I looked up to see his eyes rolling back. He pushed my head back hard to stop me from sucking him.

"Now, get on the couch and turn around."

He handled me assertively, bending me over and positioning me doggie style on the couch. My knees chafed on the cushions. I turned around to make sure he put on a condom.

"I have lube in my bag—"

"Shut up," he yelled.

He entered me forcefully. I gasped. His coarse hands were wrapped firmly around my waist, pulling me vigorously.

"Take it, you black bitch," he growled in my ear and pulled my hair tightly.

I did what I had always done as a child when I was getting fucked by a man. I tried to put my mind somewhere else.

"Oh, baby . . ." I moaned nonchalantly while praying he would come quickly.

"Shut the fuck up!"

I did as I was told. I let him have his way with me. I fought the nausea I always felt whenever a man touched me. I hated this part. Although I enjoyed the easy money, it always scarred my heart. It sent me back to those childhood memories when my mother would pimp me out to her clients so she could get her heroin fix.

My mind went back to when I was 11.

"It's okay, Sammy," Joan said, rubbing my shoulders to soothe me.

I passed the point of pleading with these random pedophiles and trying to convince them not to rape me. It felt like the more I begged them to stop, the more excited they became. I didn't want to do anything that would enhance the experience for them.

I continued to sob. It's shitty seeing your mother cheering you on when you're getting fucked to support her drug habit.

"Shut that little bitch up!" the client said.

"I'm trying, daddy. She's just a little fussy, that's all. She'll come around."

"You better try harder, bitch, or you're not getting a dime from me."

"Sammy, don't cry, baby. I know it hurts but the only way to escape the pain is to close your eyes and try not to think about it. Try to put your mind somewhere else. Imagine being with someone else . . . someone you like."

I attempted to apply her advice, but his constant tugging on my hair kept bringing me back to that hell. He turned me around onto my back. I remember feeling disgusted and appalled by him, but it went more profound than the fact that he was a man raping me. It hit me that even before I was molested regularly, every time a man touched me, even if it wasn't in a sexual way, it felt foreign. That day, I realized I was gay.

I can still smell his horrid breath and feel his clammy, thick hands groping me. I felt nauseated, inhaling that awful smell that was a mixture of musk and cologne. I listened to my mother's advice. I pictured myself in a beautiful room lying on a nice king-size bed at the Ritz-Carlton and not being raped on a barely full-sized, piss-stained mattress in a run-down room at the El Rancho Motel. Instead of the hands of a man on me, I pictured a beautiful lady's hands softly caressing me. Instead of feeling his sweaty man-boobs on me, I replaced that image with a busty woman's breasts. Instead of his cock, I imagined her thick fingers exploring me. Envisioning a woman in his place relaxed me. I noticed that I was

*no longer dry. It didn't hurt as much because my juices
began to flow while thinking about women.*

That was the only helpful advice I ever got from my
mother. She died of AIDS when I was 14. There were
conflicting stories from other prostitutes that worked
with her. Some said she got it from having unprotected
sex from selling her ass in the street, but others said she
got it by sharing needles with other fiends. Luckily for
me, I tested negative. When she died, I was left alone to
fend for myself. I sought out the Bajan pimp, Silky, who
she claimed was my father, but he wasn't buying it. I
remember approaching him one summer.

I saw a tall, thin, dark-skinned man with two beautiful
brown-skinned women holding on to each of his arms.
He was a pimp in every sense of the word. He had rollers
in his freshly permed hair, wore a black pin-striped suit
with a gaudy diamond and gold ring on his pinky finger
and glossy black alligator shoes.

I hesitated at first, pausing to contemplate my next
move. Doubt crept in the back of my mind. I wasn't sure
how he would react to me telling him that he was my
father. I wasn't sure if he would care or if he would even
acknowledge me as his daughter once he knew. Before
I could talk myself out of it, I quickly walked up to him.

"Excuse me, mister. Are you Silky?" I asked the pimp.

He licked his lips and smiled and eyed me up and
down.

"I sure am, baby doll. What's your name?"

"Samantha . . ."

"That's a pretty name for a pretty lady like yourself."

"Thanks. My mother named me after my father . . ."

He looked taken aback by my reply. His expression quickly changed. His eyes darkened. "What's your business with me, girl?"

"My mom was Joan. Your real name is Samuel Miller. My mother told me you were my daddy before she passed. I don't want anything from you. I just wanted to meet you."

Bam! The first blow hit me square on the nose, causing my eyes to well up with tears and momentarily blind me. *Bam!* The next punch split my lip. I staggered in the street trying to stop myself from falling on the ground. *Bam!* The third punch floored me. I fought to stay conscious. Groaning and groggy, I struggled to get to my feet. I could barely make out what he was yelling at me. Silky dragged me by my hair and threw me back onto the pavement. My eyes widened when I saw him pull out a switchblade. He stood over me, forcefully held my face, and pressed the knife to my throat.

"Bitch, don't you *ever* come around me again talking that shit about me being your daddy. If you think you're going to get some money out of me, you better think again."

I trembled underneath him. I instantly regretted coming down there and cursed myself for thinking it was a good idea to try to meet him.

"I don't want anything from you," I strained to say.

"Shut up, bitch."

Silky continued threatening me. "I'm going to tell you like I told your junky-ass mother. I don't *have* any fucking kids, and I don't *want* any fucking kids. If I *ever* hear you say that shit again, I'll fucking kill you. I better not hear that you been telling anyone else around here that bullshit lie either. Your junky bitch of a mother was one of my hoes; that's it. I used to fuck her now and then, but once that bitch's drug habit started growing, she was letting tricks fuck her raw for more money. She was fucking everybody, and whenever she had a slipup, she was quick to claim that a kid was mine. I'm going to tell you like I told that bitch . . . Keep my name out of your fucking mouth. Both of you bitches need to stop trying to claim me as somebody's baby daddy. I warned you this one fucking time, and I'm not going to repeat myself. Come around here again, and you're going to get hurt."

He slammed my head hard against the ground.

"Now get the fuck out of here. Keep fucking with me, and I'll bend your little ass over and break you in myself. I'll have you calling me 'daddy' for real then. Say something else, and I'll have your little ass out here selling pussy just like I had your mama and my other bitches."

Everyone on the corner stood there and watched. No one came to help me. No one tried to stop him. Like I had been all my life, I was on my own.

I wiped my eyes with the back of my hand; then I touched the back of my head and winced from the sharp pain throbbing there. When I brought my hand back to my face, it was covered in blood. I slowly rose, staggering as I ran off. Silky and his hoes were laughing at me.

Having nowhere to go, I did the only thing I knew how to do to survive. I fucked men for money. Money was the only thing I ever needed from them, and to me, it was the only thing they were good for. With my pretty face, caramel complexion, and green eyes, men always wanted a piece of me. I didn't need Silky or anyone else. I used what I had to get everything I needed. I had food to eat and clothes on my back.

Eventually, the cops caught me and shuffled me from foster home to foster home like unclaimed luggage. I met

Silka and Jaime in my first foster home, which we regularly ran away from. We bonded instantly after we shared our war stories about our shitty childhoods. We became our own little surrogate family. We protected each other. When we were hungry and needed money for food, we hustled to support each other. Silka and Jaime would shoplift from grocery stores and clothing stores to steal minor shit to survive. Jaime even sold weed occasionally, but I always ended up resorting back to prostitution because the money was quicker.

After my last stint in jail, I wanted to try to be legit for a change. I never wanted to go back to that place again. I got a job working as a cashier at an adult shop. It was the only place that would give me a chance with my record. That job got old quickly.

I was tired of dealing with managers trying to fuck me all the time and being vindictive by cutting my hours when I wouldn't let them. I was sick of breaking my back for minimum wage, being yelled at by rude-ass customers who also tried to fuck me, and coming home after two weeks with a shitty paycheck.

Back then, Cinnamon used to come by the adult shop regularly to shop for new outfits. I didn't know she was a dancer at the time. I figured she bought so many outfits because she was an escort and was selling her ass to high-profile customers. She constantly flirted with me, and while she told me the usual bullshit that she was straight, she was way too hot to pass up on trying to fuck and became my next challenge. One day, our conversation changed my life.

"You ever thought about dancing? You definitely have the body for it," Cinnamon said.

"You mean like stripping? Are you a stripper?"

She nodded. "Yup."

"Nah, that's not for me."

"All right, serious question. How much money do you make here at your little cashier job every two weeks?"

She pissed me off with that comment, so I exaggerated my two weeks' paycheck amount.

"I get about $800 every two weeks," I said, even though it was more like $500 every two weeks after taxes.

Cinnamon laughed at my answer.

"I make more than that a night at the club. You really need to drop this shitty job and make some real money dancing."

"Where do you dance?"

"I work at J's Gentlemen's Quarters on 233rd Street."

"Is the club looking for new dancers?"

She laughed. "Jerrod is always looking for fresh meat. He's the owner of the club. I already know that when he sees you, he's going to lose his mind."

"You think I have a shot of landing a spot in the club?"

"As long as you have some rhythm and you don't act all shy and shit, I can almost guarantee it. Your face is beautiful. Your body is amazing, and those two things will make men gravitate to you. Just remember the golden rule when you start working in the club. Always get the money first before you do anything with a trick," Cinnamon said.

Her words of advice sounded very similar to the rules on the street for prostitution.

"Trust me, I'm far from shy, and this wouldn't be the first time I got naked for money."

"You've danced before?"

"Something like that."

"I can see you're not going to elaborate on it, so I won't push."

"I appreciate that."

"Here, take down my number and let me get yours."

We exchanged numbers. After I achieved my goal and fucked Cinnamon a few times, her sprung ass told Jerrod about me. She set up an appointment to come in and talk to him at the club. He seemed very impressed with what he saw.

"Goddamn, girl," Jerrod said.

He hopped up from his seat and circled me, licking his lips and visually inspecting all of my curves.

"What's your name, sexy?"

"I'm Samantha. I heard y'all were looking for dancers. I want to apply for the position."

"Oh, I would love to put you in a position," he said, laughing at his own joke.

I didn't find shit funny.

"How much experience do you have as a dancer?" he asked.

"I never danced in a club setting before, but believe me when I tell you, I have plenty of experience taking my clothes off for money."

Jerrod smiled at that comment and continued looking me over from head to toe and undressing me with his eyes. He pointed and said, "There's the stage. Let me see if you got any rhythm. I hope you're not shy. Don't get performance anxiety up there. This here is your interview, so go up there and do your thing. I'll be right here checking you out."

Jerrod called out to the DJ who was in the Deejay booth getting his station ready.

"Yo, put something on for her real quick. Play something that has some pep but is also sexy."

The DJ nodded.

It was two in the afternoon, so there was only a handful of people actually by the stage, mostly old men sitting around drinking and reading the paper.

The DJ put on Kelis's "Milkshake."

Without a second thought, I jumped up on the stage.

Jerrod sat and watched my whole routine from the bar.

I felt the hard baseline from the music reverberating through the stage. I gave myself a little internal pep talk. *Bitch, you need this money. If you pull this off, you can build your money up and get an apartment instead of paying for a cheap motel room every week. You can do this. You've seen plenty of stripper routines before. All you have to do is map out in your head what you've seen them do and try to do the same shit.*

I leaned against the shiny metal pole gyrating and swaying my hips while mouthing the lyrics to the song.

I wasn't nervous at all. Dancing around naked was nothing compared to the disgusting things my mother had me do, and men requested of me when I was a kid.

I impressed Jerrod and the few men in the club with my flexibility. I sat on the wooden stage, spread my legs, raised them high, and locked them at the ankles behind my head. Then I stood up. I had taken off my top. The only thing left was my red G-string.

Three of the old men who were watching walked closer to the stage and started pulling out money.

I bent over and pulled out the side of my thong so that they could put money in it. I rubbed my breasts on one of the men's faces. He was more than thrilled. I dropped down into a split and let my ass cheeks bounce to the beat. When it was finally over, Jerrod hired me on the spot.

I hopped off the stage and walked over to the bar.

"That shit was hot! You're fucking hired."

I beamed with joy.

The DJ put on Iggy Azalea's "Work," and a white girl got on the stage and was practicing her routine. Jerrod brought my attention back to him.

"You're gonna be a fucking star. You looked like a goddess up there. You got a name picked out yet?"

I didn't, but I liked that he said I looked like a goddess, so I picked the first name that came to my mind.

"Yeah, call me Isis."

"I like that shit! Yo, Cinnamon was right about you. You can start tonight if you want to. I need someone new to put some life in this joint and hype up the crowd."

He called the white girl that was on the stage and interrupted her routine. "Yo, Vanilla. Come here."

"What do you want, Jerrod? As you can see, I'm busy trying to get ready for tonight."

"Bitch, don't question me. Bring your ass here."

She rolled her eyes and came over. She was pretty. She had bleached blond hair, huge tits, and a pair of hips and ass on her that made me question if she had some black somewhere in her family.

"Vanilla, meet Isis. Isis, this is Vanilla."

She and I gave each other small grins and limp handshakes.

"Vanilla, I need you to show Isis around the club. Show her the dressing room and make sure she has a locker. If there aren't any lockers free, tell the bitches in there that they need to work it out amongst themselves and make one available. Do you understand?"

"Yeah, I got it," Vanilla said.

Vanilla I made small talk as she showed me around. She found me a locker, introduced me to some of the strippers who were coming in early to work on their routines for the night, and talked to me about life around the club.

"While you're dancing, you want to get in the habit of dancing, but sexily and gracefully grab your money. Once your set is up, the bouncers will 'help' you collect your money quickly so the next girl can come on, and most of the time, those motherfuckers try to pocket whatever they 'help' you pick up."

"Wow, really?"

"Yup! Also, get a gym bag to put your money in and a lock for your locker. You don't want these girls taking your money when you're out on the floor trying to make more."

"I gotcha."

"Good. There are lots of ways to make money around here. You can dance your ass off, build a strong following, and make money that way. You can work the floor and build your money up doing table dances, or you can try to build your clientele up and get a lot of VIP room appearances. If you're up to it, you can fuck some of the tricks and get paid large amounts in a small amount of time. The only thing is, if you're fucking in the VIP rooms, you got to give Jerrod a cut."

I nodded. While I tried to stay away from fucking for money, this definitely beats hanging around in the street looking for johns. I knew I could easily make money here.

"Dancing is fun, but sometimes, these customers expect you to do too many tricks, and you start feeling like you're a circus act. Table dances are easy, and you can make money, but sometimes you got to work too hard to make these dudes get hard and give you more money. Me, personally, I try to do a mixture of all three. The shit has been working good for me so far. In three months, I already saved $20,000, and I'm putting a down payment on a house."

I was definitely impressed with that!

I thanked her for schooling me to how things worked around here. I called Cinnamon and told her the "interview" went well. I met up with her at her apartment and thanked her properly by fucking her brains out.

That night, I danced my ass off for the crowd. I was a natural on the stage, and the veteran strippers were throwing me shade. As Vanilla suggested, I got a small black gym bag and used it to collect my earnings from the stage.

I ran inside the dressing room, holding my bag against my chest as I leaned on my locker. The room was deserted with all of the girls on the floor trying to make their money. I emptied the bag, and the pile was mainly singles, but the denominations varied with larger bills too.

After killing it on the stage, my performance was so good that after my set, numerous men wanted lap dances and requested me for the VIP rooms.

That night alone, I made $3,000. There was no way I was going back to work for chump change at the adult shop. I didn't even give them two weeks. I just didn't show my ass there again.

That last memory brought me back to reality. Getting hired at the strip club is what brought me to this point in my life where I was being bent over and fucked in the VIP room.

Mr. Smith grunted as he came and released his grip on my hips. He slapped my ass and pulled out of me. After he was done fucking me, I felt the same queasiness and sadness that I did as a child. I got dressed, draped with the feeling of being cheap. We walked out of the room, avoiding eye contact with each other. Virginia gave him a look of disdain. The bucktoothed brother returned with their coats. Mr. Smith continued avoiding looking at me. I guess I was nothing to him now that he had gotten what he wanted from me. Virginia shook my hand.

"Thank you for a wonderful evening, darling," she said, then discreetly slipped me a small ivory-colored business card.

I palmed it, hiding it from view, and nodded as they headed out the door. After they were gone, I walked toward the dressing room.

"Isis!" Jerrod, the club manager, called out.

He was an arrogant prick who always sported a gold tooth and different color velour jumpsuits. This day he wore a black-and-white Adidas jumpsuit with a matching pair of crisp white shell-top kicks. His father had been accidentally killed on a construction site in Manhattan. His family sued the city, and he used his part of the money he received to open this shithole.

I ignored him and kept on walking.

"Bitch, I know you hear me calling you," he yelled.

I didn't know who the fuck he thought he was, but he was way too loose with calling all the strippers bitches, so I fucked with him out of retaliation every chance I got.

I rolled my eyes and turned around. "What?" I was in no mood to talk to his ass, but I was taken aback by who he had with him.

"First off, calm yourself when you talk to me. Second, give me my cut from that couple you were with."

I reached in my Prada wristlet wallet, put in the card that Virginia gave me, and handed him the $500 I had separated from my earnings earlier. A huge smile grew on his face.

"Who's the cutie with you?" I inquired.

"This is Sasha. Cinnamon recommended her. She's going to be our hostess and help out with other shit around here. When shit is slow, she'll act as our one of our cocktail waitresses and bring drinks to customers at their tables. When it's busy, she'll be helping Jaime out with bartending."

Sasha was stunning. Her chestnut eyes, smooth chocolate complexion, and banging body drew me to her. She looked noticeably out of place. She had an innocent air about her that accentuated her beauty to me.

I looked her up and down. Her hard nipples protruded from her white Baby Phat T-shirt, which provided a nice snug fit that showcased her full C-cup breasts.

Jerrod licked his lips. "I'm trying to convince her to dance. She definitely has the body for it, but she keeps telling me no. I think she would make a lot of money for both of us if she did," he said.

She rolled her eyes, playfully waved him off, and laughed. "Hi, Isis. I watched your set. You were killing them out there."

She reached out to shake my hand.

I lifted her hand and kissed it.

"I'm glad you enjoyed it, shorty. Call me Sam. Maybe one day, I'll give you a private show."

"Nah, cut that shit out right now," Jerrod said. "You ain't gonna be fucking every new piece of ass I bring in here. That shit is bad for business and hurts my pockets when they quit because you broke their little hearts."

Sasha laughed again. "It's okay. Trust me; I'm not going to be a statistic. I have a man at home that holds it down in the bedroom. I won't be switching teams any time soon," she said confidently.

"If I hadn't heard that line before, I would believe it. But this bitch got superpowers or some shit. I've seen many girls talk the same shit you're talkin' and then get turned out. She's that good."

She turned toward me, and our eyes connected. I confidently held my gaze until she blushed and looked away. I wasn't mad about Jerrod clit blocking. What neither of them realized is that his warning about my notoriety would actually help to spark her curiosity and make my seduction of her easier. I smiled to myself.

"Sasha, it was nice meeting you. I hope this taint hasn't soiled my good name too much. Hopefully, we can become friends."

"Who are you calling a taint? Watch it, bitch," Jerrod said, frowning at me.

Sasha laughed at our squabbling. "I'd like that," she responded.

I winked at her.

"You have a good night, and if you have any questions about this place, don't hesitate to ask me."

I looked Jerrod up and down, rolled my eyes, and said, "Later, nigga."

He waved me off. I stepped on his sneakers as I walked past him to go to the dressing room.

"Bitch, you need to stop playing. You scuffed my shit."

Ignoring him, I entered the dressing room. Cinnamon was sitting at one of the pink and black vanity tables putting on her makeup. Her real name was Cindy, and she had a golden complexion with a huge bubble butt. She was wearing a gold G-string that clung to her pussy lips with a matching bra that showcased her double-D breasts. She had black pasties on underneath her bra that covered her pierced nipples and had blond highlighted streaks that ran down her hair that was in a ponytail. We fooled around sexually a couple of times in the past, but nothing serious. At the time, she was a challenge, and after I conquered that challenge, I wasn't interested anymore. She was a good sport though and didn't take it personally. We've always been friendly with each other.

"Hey, Cinnamon, that new girl Sasha is your friend, right?"

"Yeah, girl, and hands off, you vulture. She is strictly dickly."

"That's what they all say."

"I've known her since junior high school, and we go to college together now. Trust me, she a churchgoing girl. She's not interested," Cinnamon said, adjusting her boobs and cleavage in her bra. She gave herself a once-over and winked at herself in approval.

"Yeah, yeah. From my experience, churchgoers are always the biggest sinners. You cool with her?" I asked.

"She's not my homegirl like that. We're not having sleepovers at each other's houses and shit, but we're friendly. We hang out together every once in a while."

"All right, cool. Tell me about her."

"Damn, why are you so thirsty for her already? You just met her."

"I'm always interested in learning about my newest coworkers, that's all."

"Yeah, you're full of shit. You're always interested in fucking the new 'meat.' You did the same shit when Sapphire started working here and any other pretty face that walks in this dressing room."

When Cinnamon said that, Sapphire, who was getting ready for her set, gave both of us dirty looks before walking up to me.

"You don't need to play with that little girl. If you want to have fun, you got a grown woman right here. You *know* I'm always down."

I rolled my eyes at her. "Bitch, please. Ho, be gone."

She huffed, gave me a venomous look, and stormed out of the dressing room.

Sapphire's real name was Sophia. I turned her out within the first month of her working at the club. At the time, she had a boyfriend. I thought she was sexy as hell. I loved the challenge, but after I beat that, as usual, I lost interest. She thought since we fucked a few times, we would have a connection and become something in the future. But I was blunt and explained to her that what we had was nothing more than a good time. She had been pissed at me ever since, but I didn't give a shit. Despite everything, she was still in my face, constantly trying to convince me to fuck her again.

"C'mon, give me the rundown on this chick," I said playfully to Cinnamon.

"She has a boyfriend named Travis who she lives with around 165th and Jerome Avenue. They've been dating off and on for the longest, but I think he's just an unemployed pothead who uses her. She can do so much better."

So far, the information she was telling me was golden. All I needed was the right approach to come at her.

"She goes to school with me at Lehman College for graphic design. She wants to edit photos for a major magazine one day."

That was something that we had in common that I could use to get me close to her. Once I shared my passion for photography with her, and we bonded over the arts, there was no way I couldn't bag her.

"Why would she want to work here? I saw it in her face. She's as green as they come. She's definitely not built to handle things in this type of environment," I said.

"She's here for the same reason a lot of us are here. She's here because between paying for tuition, books, supporting herself, and her broke-ass boyfriend, she needed the extra money to survive. I should get a finder's fee for all the recruitment I do for this damn place. I told her that she could work here a couple of nights and make a few dollars off tips. Jerrod was trying to get her to dance, but she wasn't having that. Like I said before, she's really religious."

"Thanks, Cin. I learned everything I needed to know."

"Seriously, Isis, don't fuck her over. She's a good girl."

"I'll be gentle," I said, winking at her.

"I don't want you to hurt her like you hurt Sapphire and the other girls here."

"Did I hurt you?"

"I'm different. I knew what it was and what I was getting myself into. I enjoyed what we had while it lasted. I was smart enough to know it wouldn't last forever. I'm more street smart than Sapphire and Sasha. Don't hurt her."

"Cin, I can't promise you that, but I'll do my best."

I reapplied my makeup and prepared myself to head back out to the stage for my next set. If Sasha enjoyed the performance I was about to put on for those losers, she had no idea what I had planned to seduce her.

Three

Wants and Needs

"I'm so tired of this shit," Jaime said, putting her head down and weeping.

Silka rubbed Jaime's shoulders and moved her braids out of her face as tears streamed down her butterscotch skin. We were all sitting in my apartment listening to Jaime vent over being laid off from yet another job.

"I know this shit has to do with me doing a bid at Rikers. I shouldn't have lied about it on the application, but when you're honest and tell people you did a little jail time in the past, they don't give you a fair chance. They think once a criminal, always a criminal, and you're incapable of changing for the better."

Jaime slammed her fist down on my wooden coffee table. I understood her frustration. While we all had our run-ins with the law, only Jaime and I had been to jail. I had gone for prostitution; Jaime did a stint for grand larceny and drug possession. Our records hindered us from getting most jobs, so we always did what we had to do to survive. Silka was always a bookworm. Even though she did some dirt in the past, she always did well in school. After she got picked up a couple of times by the cops for shoplifting, she stopped, kept her head in the books, got full academic scholarships, and went to Fordham

University for her undergraduate and graduate degrees. I had never been a model student, but I held my own when it came to taking classes. I, at least, had my GED. For Jaime, she didn't have the patience to get her GED, which was another blemish that hurt her chances of landing a decent-paying job. I got her the bartending gig at the strip club with me, but that was only meant to supplement her income with the job she already had, not be her main source. There was no way she could live on that pay and tips alone.

I handed Jaime some tissues. She wiped her face.

"I'm so fucked right now. I can't even afford to keep my shitty-ass studio apartment."

"You know you can always stay with me. It would be tight in my place, but you can stay with Georgia, Dom, and me. We would be roommates again like back in the day," Silka said.

"I appreciate that, and I'm grateful, sis, but I couldn't do that to you. You have a family, and I would just be in the way," Jaime replied.

"If you find yourself really hitting rock bottom, drop your apartment and stay with me," I offered.

"Thanks, but I got to try to do this shit on my own. I hope I don't have to eat my words and take you up on your offer."

"You and Silka are the only family I have. I would do anything for you guys," I said.

We all shared in a sisterly hug.

"All right, girls, I have to head home. Dom has plans with his boys tonight," Silka said.

"You better watch him. You know men can't be trusted. Who knows what he does when he's out with them," I added.

"He could say the same thing when I hang out with you two. You have to learn to trust men. They aren't all bad, you know. You, of all people, know that a woman can fuck you up just as bad as a man."

I flipped her off as she picked up her purse.

"I got to head out too. I'm going to ask Jerrod if I can work seven days a week bartending at the club for the extra money," Jaime said.

"Why don't you ask him if you can start dancing?" I said.

"Not all of us are blessed with a perfect body like you," she stated.

Jaime wasn't obese, but she wasn't thin either. She had some size to her. Still, she had curves that made people turn their heads. Jaime had a beautiful set of long, thick legs with a firm ass that protruded like you could set a tray on it. To maximize on tips when she bartended, she always wore push-up bras that pronounced her 32 double-D breasts beautifully. She had a bit of a tummy, but nothing that a few days a week in the gym couldn't fix.

"I'm sorry, but I could never be comfortable with a bunch of horny-ass men and women, feeling up on me, calling me names, smacking me on the ass, and trying to finger fuck me all night," Jaime said.

"Well, that explains why you don't have a dating life," I joked.

We laughed as she continued.

"But seriously, I need money, but not that bad . . . no offense."

"None taken. To each, her own."

"On that note, I got to go. Silka, I'll walk out with you," Jaime said.

Silka nodded, and we said our goodbyes.

After they left, I listened to the messages on my voice-mail from random women I had fucked who were either wondering why I hadn't called or begging me to see them again. I laughed to myself. On my desk, I saw the card from Mrs. Smith. I thought about ripping it up and throwing it out, but something told me to hold off and not burn that bridge just yet. She had money, so I knew I could easily fuck her brains out and squeeze some more cash out of her. This card could definitely come in handy.

I toyed with the idea of calling Virginia. Reading the number off the card, I decided to call her and see what the deal was with that.

"Hello," Virginia answered.

"Um . . . hi . . . this is . . . uh . . . Isis."

Virginia lowered her voice. "From the strip club, right?" she asked.

"Yeah . . ."

"I've been hoping you would call me. I really enjoyed our time together, and I want to see you again. I can make it worth your while."

If she was already talking like that, I knew I could easily get some money out of her. As soon as I'd get her to my apartment, I knew I'd fuck her brains out.

"I'm listening. What do you mean by that?" I inquired.

"My husband and I are powerful people. Name your price, and we can help each other."

We talked more about meeting up, and before I knew it, she was at my door.

"Just a minute," I yelled.

I had on a black lace bustier with stockings. I quickly grabbed my silk robe out of the bathroom, put it on, and headed to the door.

"Hey," I said, stepping to the side so she could walk into my place.

"Hello, darling. It's good to see you again."

Virginia's eyes traveled around my apartment. She looked out of place in my neighborhood with her expensive clothes and jewelry.

"Did you have trouble finding my apartment?" I asked.

"No. There's no place I can't find with my GPS," she joked.

"I have to ask you this. What's the catch? Why are you so interested in me?"

She looked as if she were trying to put together the right words to help me understand.

"I've seen a lot of strippers. I've slept with a lot of women, but none of them have left me craving for more like you did. It's scary because I can see myself getting addicted to you."

I laughed to myself. "Is that right?"

"Yes."

"Are you gay?"

"I'm married to Wall Street royalty. In the position I'm in, I can't afford to be gay. I do what I must to keep myself happy and satisfied."

"So, your marriage is just for show?"

I don't think she had ever thought of it in that way because her expression momentarily changed to one of confusion. She shook it off and said, "Our marriage is more for financial purposes than for love. He could never be completely faithful to me, anyway. I've caught him plenty of times fucking other women. At least now he doesn't do it behind my back. We share women."

"So, he knows that you want to get fucked by girls on a regular basis?"

"Why do you think we went to your club? My husband, Marcus, wanted to find a nice 'urban' spot where we could both enjoy a beautiful woman. Our new driver, Tyrone, said he knew of a place that might interest us."

"So, by 'urban,' do you mean black?"

"Bluntly, yes. I'm attracted to women of color."

Her eyes canvassed my place more. I'm sure she wasn't used to such a modest apartment.

"Your place is . . . cute," Virginia said.

"Thanks. It's not much, and it's probably not up to your standards or what you're used to, but it's all mine. Everything in here, including my apartment, I paid for, and I take pride in it."

"No judgment, dear. You're pride and spunk is what draws me to you. So . . . Do you like what you do?"

"It's all right. I just view it as a means to get by for now. It pays the bills."

"Why do you work at that strip club in the middle of that . . . that neighborhood? You would make a hell of a lot more money if you worked in a more upscale place. You're way too beautiful to be in such a wretched place."

"I like it there. I make decent money, and I don't plan on being there forever anyway," I said while rolling my eyes at her comment.

"Oh, what are your plans, darling? I'm glad you realize that a stripping career has a very short life span."

She had a snobbish air about her that attracted me and irritated me at the same time. Her pompous attitude only made me want to fuck her even more.

"Right now, I have a small photography business that I run out of my apartment. I do all types of portraits, make portfolios, and do a little videography, as well. Eventually, I plan on opening a studio and quitting this stripper shit."

I knew why she was here, and I knew what she desired. I wanted to skip all the bullshit and get straight to the point. Virginia was accustomed to people kissing her ass and doing whatever she wanted. I've dealt with her type before. What she truly craved was to be dominated by a woman.

"Look, I know why you're here, Virginia. We can skip the small talk and get down to business."

"Is that right? Why do you think I'm here?"

She stood next to my window. I walked up close to her and said, "Strip."

"Pardon me?" Virginia said.

"Did I stutter? You heard what I said. Take off your clothes now. I'm not going to tell you again. We both know why you're here."

A naughty grin came across her face. She slowly took off her blouse and bra.

"Take off the rest," I commanded.

She laughed and did as she was told.

"Good girl," I said.

I pushed her back against the window, grabbed her hands, and pressed them over her head. She looked scared and excited at the same time. I enjoyed the look of uncertainty and fear on her face as she stood there trembling.

"What are you going to do to me?" she asked.

"Shut up."

"Aren't you going to close the blinds at least? I'm naked in front of your window."

"I said, shut up. If you keep talking, I'm going to gag you. Keep your hands up and don't move."

She smiled. I knew this was what she wanted. I cupped her breasts and pushed them together while I licked around her areolas. Virginia moaned and threw her head back. She put her hands on top of my head and attempted to force me to go down on her. I batted her hands away.

"Look here, 'Mrs. Smith,' in this place, *I* run shit. You will do what *I* say when *I* say it, or I'll punish you. Do we understand each other?"

She nodded.

"Good."

I got down on my knees, licked my middle finger, and stuck it inside of her. I curved my finger and moved it in a circular motion against the top of her vagina, massaging her G-spot. Virginia closed her eyes. Her body moved to the rhythm of my hand. I removed my finger, gripped her ass, and tugged her closer to me. I licked and hummed on her vagina while simultaneously rubbing against her G-spot. I felt her knees buckle.

"Oh God . . ." she moaned.

I rose up from the floor and walked her over to my bedroom, where I pushed her down onto her back on the mattress. I watched as she slid her toned body backward up my bed. She stretched out her legs and propped herself into a reclined position on her elbows.

"You're so intense," she said, trying to collect her breath.

"Put your hands up and hold on to that bedpost."

"What?"

I lifted her legs and slapped her ass.

Smack!

"Don't play with me. You heard what I said."

Virginia extended her arms upward until her hands were wrapped around the middle bedpost on the headboard.

"What are you going to do to me?" She quivered as our eyes met.

"Shut up and stop asking questions."

I walked to my closet and pulled out a pair of hand-cuffs and leg shackles.

I cuffed her wrists to the bedpost and shackled her legs to the sides of my bed. She tugged, struggled, and strained to get free, but it wasn't happening. They weren't furry novelty cuffs, either. My cuffs and leg shackles were official police grade that I bought from a retired cop off craigslist.

"Relax, I'm not going to hurt you," I said calmly.

Her pussy was so unbelievably wet; I could see the moisture coating her inner thighs.

I trailed my left index finger up her legs, running my fingers over her breasts, and then I grabbed her by the throat.

Virginia gagged a little. Her body tensed. There was fear in her eyes as she wiggled in the cuffs, powerless to stop me.

I fingered her pussy relentlessly while I mildly choked her. She arched her back.

"I'm so close . . . so fucking close. Don't stop," she said.

I stopped what I was doing. She whimpered.

"Please . . . please—"

"Please what?" I asked grinning.

"Please keep fucking me."

"You want me to keep going?"

She nodded.

I smiled. "Good! I got something for you."

I stood up and walked back to my closet. Her seduc-tive eyes watched my every move.

I grabbed a bag filled with my sex toys and threw it on the bed. Then I pulled a blindfold out of the bag and put it over her eyes.

"Why do I have to be blindfolded?" she asked.

"Didn't I tell you to shut up and stop asking questions? You're two seconds away from being gagged. I'll do whatever I want to you, do you understand?"

"Yes."

I pulled out a butt plug, my rabbit vibrator, and massaging wand. I poured the lube on the butt plug. She jumped as I lubed up her anus and worked my index finger in it to prepare her for the butt plug. I slowly inserted the plug into her ass. I worked my fingers inside her flower; then I replaced my fingers with my rabbit vibrator, gradually increasing the speed.

"Oh my God!" she moaned.

I continued working the vibrator into her wetness with my left hand while I simultaneously and discreetly worked the buttons on my massaging wand with my right hand. Her breathing was quickening. Her mouth was opening wide. From the look of things on her blindfolded face, my actions were building her closer to her peak with every thrust and turn of the vibrator.

Virginia was already being pushed to the limits with the rabbit, but I wanted her to have a volcanic orgasm. Without notice, I placed the wand directly on her clitoris.

"Fuck, fuck, fuck!" she whimpered over and over again.

"You like that? You like getting fucked like this?" I asked.

She was so lost in the feeling of euphoria that she couldn't even respond to my questions.

Her legs were shaking uncontrollably. Her breathing sounded like she was hyperventilating. Virginia bit her bottom lip and bucked so hard from coming that I thought she would break free from her restraints. Afterward, she lay limp on the bed twitching.

"I've never been fucked like that. Ever!" she said, out of breath.

I smiled to myself. "The night isn't over. I didn't say I was done with you yet. As long as you're still in those restraints, your ass is mine! You got that?"

She smiled and said, "Yes, Isis."

"Damn skippy."

I continued to fuck her brains out the rest of that evening. I enjoyed making her arrogant ass come under my control. I felt nothing for her, but if I could use her money and connections to get my business off the ground, I would do whatever I needed to.

I strutted onto the stage and gyrated to the music as I rolled my shapely hips while leaning against the shining metal pole and mouthing the words to David Guetta's "Sexy Bitch." Here, on this stage, I had the power. I shimmied and squeezed my breasts together with my arms while pinching my nipples. I flicked the tip of my tongue and traced my right areola while cupping my breasts. Then I tilted my head back, seductively looking over my shoulder at the audience. My body was on point! I've always known this, but what truly drew people to me were my deep green, almond-shaped eyes. I kept my gaze focused on the crowd as I swayed my hips.

"Work that shit, Isis!" one man yelled.

I walked around the pole, working my magic. A heavy-set man held up five crisp, one-dollar bills. I sauntered to the end of the stage, smiled as I eased down to the floor, crawled over seductively, and pulled on the sides of my pink G-string to collect my money. Seductively, I writhed around on the floor, gyrated my hips, and spread my legs to give them a good view of my honey pot.

"Goddamn! She's killin' it tonight," I heard someone say. When I'm onstage, the rush I get is incredible. The money is quick and easy.

I looked into the crowd and saw Sasha leaned against the bar, staring at me, watching my every move. She ignored the customers who were trying to get her attention.

I stood up and bent over again as I grabbed my ankles, wiggled, and showed off my firm ass. I slapped the sides of my cheeks and rubbed my hands down my thighs. When the song ended, I walked around the stage quickly to pick up the remainder of my money, while flirting with customers to try to finagle more cash out of them.

Finished, I walked through the curtains and made my way to the dressing room where I freshened up, changed outfits, and then headed to the floor. Out of the corner of my eye, I saw Sasha was talking to Jaime at the bar. I already schooled Jaime about my intentions for Sasha, so she knew to assist in any way she could to make my courting easier. Jaime wasn't gay, but she always looked out for me and vice versa.

"What are you guys talking about over here?" I asked.
Sasha jumped.

"We were actually talking about you," Jaime replied.

"Were you now? Good things, I hope."

"Always! Come on, you know we're family."

I winked at Jaime and mouthed "thank you" when Sasha wasn't looking.

"It's nice to know that I'm so important," I said, smiling.

Jaime chuckled.

"Sasha here was telling me how she thought your performance was all that."

"Did she now?" I said, standing close to her, purposely invading her personal space.

I looked at Sasha. She blushed.

"You were on fire with your performance up there. Forget Shakira. Your hips don't lie," Sasha laughed.

"You have no idea what these hips can do, but I would love to show you sometime," I stated flirtatiously.

"I got to go service these thirsty niggas. I'll leave you two to talk," Jaime said.

Jaime made drinks for the customers at the bar while I talked to Sasha.

"So, I hear you're going to school for graphic design. You know I'm a photographer, right?"

"You're a photographer?" she asked with a look of disbelief.

"Yes. There's more to me than 'Isis.' You should get to know me. What are you doing after work?"

"Going home and resting up. I had a long week."

"Stop by my place and check out my work."

I could see in her face that she didn't trust me. Her uneasiness made my suspicions stronger that there was something there. It was becoming apparent she didn't trust herself.

"I don't know. When we get out of here, it's going to be late. I really need to get home to my man."

"Look, nothing is going to happen that you don't want to happen. I'm not going to push myself on you if you're worried about that. Despite what you might believe, I actually have a legit photography business."

She looked torn as if she didn't know what to do.

"Okay, I'll stop by for a little bit after work to check you out . . . I mean . . . check your work out, not you," she stammered.

I smiled to myself. "I know what you meant. It's cool."

After we finished working, Sasha followed me to my place. My strategy was a simple one—gain her trust. Once she got to know me, her true nature would run its course.

"Your apartment is so nice," she said.

"Thanks!"

I pulled out four huge albums of my work to show her. She looked at each picture in amazement.

"Wow! Did you *really* do these?"

"Yup."

"They're amazing. You have talent with a camera."

"Thank you."

As I thought, our common interest in photography gave me the opening I needed to chitchat and get to know her. She was an interesting woman. She supported herself and her boyfriend and dreamt of making it big in the graphic arts world. I usually couldn't stand the women I fucked, but I put up with their shit.

With Sasha, things were different. She wasn't a bird like the usual women I hunted. She was smart. I enjoyed talking to her. She was hardworking and ambitious. Her innocence engrossed me. The world hadn't completely fucked her over yet, so she was still green when it came to seeing how manipulative people could be. In a way, I liked that. I had been fucked over so many times, that it was cute seeing someone that still saw beauty in an ugly world.

"Damn, it's so late. I have to start heading home. I can't believe we've been talking for so long," she said.

I looked at her intently and held her hand.

"Time flies when you're having fun. You should hang out with me more often."

"I did enjoy kicking it with you tonight. We should hang out again . . . Your eyes are really pretty. I'm sorry. I don't know if that came out weird. I'm not that way."

I laughed to myself. The attraction was there. With a little patience, she would conform.

"It's okay. Not to sound big-headed, but I get that a lot."

"I bet."

"What's up with us talking more? Can I call you sometime? Here, put your number in my phone so that we can keep in touch."

We exchanged numbers, promised that we would definitely hang out again, and I walked her out. Things would take time, but the end result would be the same. She would be mine.

Four

Company

"Get ready!" I said.

Virginia was bent over on all fours on my bed with my red ball gag shoved in her mouth. I wore my strap—a ten-inch long, three-inch wide dildo that I named "Big Black." I tightened the leather harness, making minor adjustments so that it fit just right. Satisfied, I poured lube and rubbed it amply on the head and shaft of the dildo. I did the same with her vagina. I worked my fingers in and out to tease her, preparing her for the big surprise. I didn't always use straps, but for this bitch, I wanted to hear her scream and leave her sore.

The best part of our sessions was the spontaneity. I had no plan, rhyme, or reason to how I was going to fuck her, and to me, that was the beauty of it.

"Now listen to me very carefully 'cause I'm only going to say this once. You better not take your eyes off that fucking headboard. If I see your eyes move from that spot, I'll punish you. You understand? Nod your head if you understand what the fuck I'm telling you."

Virginia quickly nodded.

I squirted lube down the small of her back and watched it drip down the crack of her ass to her vagina. A shiver traveled the length of her spine when I followed up with my fingers. I ran the smooth dildo up and down her entrance while cupping her breasts in my hands. I pinched her nipples as she wiggled her ass, eager to be penetrated.

"Do you want me to fuck you?"

Virginia nodded.

I grabbed the base of the strap-on and shoved it into her pussy.

She grunted and yelped through the ball gag as I tugged on her hair and pounded her as fast and as hard as I could.

I yanked her hair with my left hand, took hold of her right hip with my right hand, and continuously stroked her. Virginia's loud moans and the slapping sound of her ass against my leather strap echoed throughout the room.

Unlike men, I didn't get tired from working my hips. I wouldn't be a two-pump chump and come prematurely. As a dancer, gyrating my hips was second nature to me. I could please her all day.

My pelvis collided with her ass with every movement. I held her wrists behind her back with one hand and slapped her ass cheeks in quick succession with the other. Her ass turned a bright pink complexion as her butt bounced and wiggled with each smack.

Virginia played with her clit and threw her ass back at me, begging me for more while I hammered her mercilessly from behind.

The sounds of her muffled moans, the sight of the rippling orgasms rushing through her, and the feel of her moist body against mine turned me on. I loved watching her grasp the sheets; she twisted them in knots and bit down on the gag while I penetrated her relentlessly. I felt so powerful. Seeing her helpless to stop my unyielding pounding made me feel like a god. While I was extremely

rough with her, she loved every minute of it. I knew I was
going to have this bitch hooked.

Virginia was a godsend. She kept my pockets filled
with money every time I saw her, and she was my savior
when it came to improving my photography business. At
first, I felt she was just being a bitch when critiquing my
portraits.

"Your work is . . . nice, but if you want to be taken
seriously, darling, you have to have better equipment."

"What's wrong with the stuff I have?" I asked, offended by her statement.

"Your stuff is adequate for amateur work, but if you
want to be taken seriously and make it in the business,
you must have better equipment. A nice eye for photography will make you good, but the proper equipment will
make you great."

I didn't care for her comments, but the next day,
Virginia presented me with a Canon 1DX camera—one
of the top professional cameras on the market.

"For you, darling," she said, smiling at me.

"What? You didn't have to do this," I said.

"I believe the correct response is thank you."

"Thank you."

"Now, look in the hallway."

On the floor in big plastic J&R Electronic bags were
macrolenses, wide-angle lenses, and zoom lenses. She
also bought me lighting gear, lighting boxes, soft light
kits, studio kits, tripods, backdrops, and a Mac computer
and laptop fully loaded with all types of photo manage-
ment software to organize all my pictures so I could run
my business more efficiently.

Virginia referred me to some of her rich hipster friends, paid for a website to be created for me, placed ads in local newspapers and magazines, and had business cards made for me. Her friends thought it was so avant-garde that I ran my studio out of my quaint apartment. I put away the money that Virginia was giving me and the extra I made from the portraits in a savings account. My dream of saving to expand and open a legit studio was becoming a reality.

While things were going great for me, Jaime was struggling worse than before. I needed to find a way to help my girl, and Virginia was the key to that. One day after I sexed her up good, I asked her for her help with Jaime.

"Can I ask you for a favor?"

Virginia sat naked on my bed, smoking a cigarette looking refreshed and rejuvenated. "That depends on what it is. What would be the favor?"

"Can you use your connections to help my friend, Jaime, with a job?"

"Does she have a résumé? How much education does she have?"

I gave Virginia the whole rundown on Jaime. She was a little reluctant at first, but she eventually gave in and found Jaime a job as an administrative assistant for a law firm close to Wall Street. Virginia had to lie big time on Jaime's résumé—and pull a lot of strings—but Jaime got the job.

"Thank you, thank you, thank you!" Jaime said to Virginia and me excitedly.

I hugged her. Virginia gave her a curt smile.

"I have to go home and figure out what I'm going to wear tomorrow for my first day. I honestly can't thank you two enough. I really appreciate this," Jaime said.

"You know I always got your back. You're my sister," I told her.

"And I always have yours too. You know this," Jaime responded.

I walked her out.

"Please tell your friend to be on her best behavior. I can't have her acting wildly and ruining my reputation. If my husband found out, there would be no way to explain why I pushed for Jaime to get that job," Virginia said.

"Relax. She knows how to act. She wouldn't do anything stupid to jeopardize her job; she needs it too much. Now shut up, take off your clothes, and let me thank you properly."

Things were looking up. All I needed now was to finish seducing Sasha, and everything would be perfect!

The rain came down in buckets. I stood underneath the awning of the strip club and took long drags of my cigarette to relax before heading back inside for two more hours of being groped and gawked at. Now that my photography business had picked up, doing that and working at this shithole felt like I was burning my candle at both ends. I was cranky, tired, and felt like my monthly visitor would arrive soon.

"Damn, baby! What are you doing out here all alone? You want some company?" a random man asked.

I ignored him, rolled my eyes, and waved him away. I looked off toward the parking lot while he continued trying to kick game to me. Spotting Sasha sitting in her car crying, I flicked my cigarette and dashed in the direction of her car.

"Hey, can I get your number?" the guy yelled.

"I'm seeing someone," I lied.

"So?"

"I don't get down like that."

"Whatever, bitch."

I laughed at him and knocked on Sasha's window.

"You all right in there?" I asked.

She slouched down in her car and rolled the window down. "Yes, I'm okay. I just need to be alone right now."

"What happened? What's wrong?" I asked.

"Nothing. I just really need to be alone."

Although soaked, I wanted to capitalize on this opportunity. She was vulnerable right now. So I saw it as the perfect chance to gain her trust and make progress on bedding her.

"Sasha, I'm not going to leave you out here crying. Are you going to tell me what's going on?"

"Sam, please, just let me be."

"Nope. Are you going to be rude and leave me standing here in the rain or are you at least going to unlock your passenger-side door so I can sit in your car and talk to you?"

Sasha sighed. She picked up a couple of books that were on the passenger's seat, reached over, and unlocked the door for me. I walked to the passenger side and got in. Our eyes met. Her soft brown eyes glistened with tears. I used my thumbs to wipe them from her face gently. My tan trench coat was open, showing the black lace lingerie I was wearing from my last set. Sasha stared at my body, then turned her head when she realized I noticed.

"You don't want to hear my bullshit. It will only sound stupid to you. Correction, it will only reinforce your feelings about men," Sasha said.

"If you're bothered by it, it won't sound stupid to me. I've always had a strong disdain for men. Nothing you tell me is going to change how I already feel."

"I can't take it anymore."

"What's on your mind, ma? What's stressing you like this?"

"I feel like my life is falling apart."

Her hands were on her lap. I rested my hands on top of hers and gave her a warm, caring smile. She didn't flip out or pull away. She stayed calm and collected.

"Start from the beginning," I told her.

"Where do I begin? I'm drowning in debt. I work so much that I'm not studying as much as I should be, and I'm failing two classes. If that weren't enough, I caught my man fucking some bitch in my apartment."

"Damn! What did he say when you caught him?"

"I ran after the girl to kick her ass. He held me down while she got dressed and ran off. We argued, and I asked him why he cheated. He said at times, he feels like I emasculate him, and he wanted a woman to treat him like a man. I told him if he wanted me to treat him like that, he should get a job and stop leaving all the pressure of supporting us on me. That pissed him off. He told me that he was leaving me for her." Sasha started crying again. "I can't talk to my family about this. They hated him from the beginning. I can't go home. I can't watch him packing the shit that I bought him."

"It's okay. I'm here for you," I said, consoling her.

"Seriously, don't worry about me. Go in there and make your money."

"Those thirsty niggas can wait. You're more important to me than them."

Sasha smiled.

"Hang out at my place after work."

"I don't know . . ."

"Are you still worried about me trying to touch you?"

"Kind of."

"Did I try to touch you last time?"

"No."

"I'm definitely attracted to you, but I don't force myself on women. You're hurting, and I want to be there for you. That's all."

"Okay."

Sasha made it clear she wasn't going to stay long. Knowing me, I would probably be horny afterward and go out again looking to fuck some chick, so I told her to leave her car at the club. She rode with me to my place. As we walked into my apartment, I got a text from Sapphire.

Sapphire: Want some company tonight?

Me: I do, but not from you.

She responded with a sad face. I ignored her bullshit and focused on Sasha.

I made us Patrón shots and let her vent to me. By her fifth shot, Sasha was a complete chatterbox, telling me every little detail about her life. She told me about her on-again, off-again relationship with her man, and her super-religious family.

"So, tell me more about your family," I said.

"What do you want to know?"

"Start with the basics."

"I'm the oldest of four children. I have two brothers, Jimmy and Joseph, and a sister named Josephine."

I waved my hand, motioning for her to continue.

"My dad is a pastor at a church he runs in Brooklyn. My mom helps him out at the church and takes care of the house."

"Ugh! So, your father turned your mother into a domesticated breeder, huh?"

Sasha laughed. "My mom loves her life. Taking care of her family makes her happy."

I could've gone on a tirade about how typical it was for men to trick women by blinding them with children and nice houses. They slowed women down to try to keep that false sense of supremacy. I wanted to explain how men created that illusion to make women believe they were happy, but the reality was that men trapped women. It's no different than slavery. While I had these feelings, I kept my comments to myself.

"Are you religious?" Sasha asked.

"Nope, not at all. Most religions don't take kindly to my lifestyle."

Sasha had a weird expression on her face.

"Do you think because of your . . . um . . . lifestyle that you are not going to go to heaven?"

"I don't believe in heaven."

"Do you believe in God?"

"I honestly don't know. I had a rough life growing up. If there is a God, I wonder what I did to deserve the childhood I had."

"What happened during your childhood?"

Telling someone I desired about my childhood wasn't sexy. I didn't want her to pity me, and there was no way she wouldn't if she heard about my junkie prostitute mother allowing men to rape me as a child. I wasn't proud of my upbringing. In short, I was embarrassed about it. Rather than bring back terrible memories for me and have her compare our different childhoods, I redirected the conversation back to her.

"We'll talk about me when the time is right. Right now, I want to know all about you."

I handed her another drink.

"Nope, I want to know more about you. Why do you have 'pain is love' tattooed on your side?"

"I have a quirky philosophy when it comes to love. I believe the ones you love the most hurt you the deepest. My tattoo helps me never to forget why I feel that way."

"Do you want to talk about that?"

I chuckled and said, "Nope."

"Okay, well, since I told you about my family, tell me about yours."

I sighed. "There's nothing to talk about there. I don't have one. My mother, Joan, was a junkie prostitute who died of AIDS when I was 14. My father, Silky, was a pimp who denied I was his daughter and left me to fend for myself in the street. He was killed around the time of my seventeenth birthday by one of his hoes."

Talking about my past was working my nerves. I fired up a cigarette. Sasha fanned the smoke away.

"Sorry. I'll take a few more drags, then put it out."

"They're so unhealthy, you know."

"Yeah, well, I need them. They calm my nerves."

"Does talking about your past make you uncomfortable? I understand if you don't want to talk about it with me yet. All I'll say is God doesn't give us more than we can handle. Look at your life like this . . . You wouldn't be who you are today if you didn't experience the things in your past."

"I've had more shit happen to me during my childhood than most people have in their lifetime. Where was God then? That's how I know God is a man. Why didn't He help me when I needed Him the most? Because He's useless."

Where did that come from? Feeling myself getting emotional, I shook it off.

"I know you might've experienced a lot of pain, but God helps with all of our problems if you believe in Him."

I laughed to myself. "I guess I need to see the blessing first before I start believing in anything."

"I'm going to tell you something that I have never told anyone else. I think you'll appreciate it."

My face lit up like a Christmas tree. I smiled and prayed she would tell me that she was secretly a lesbian or at least bisexual.

"I'm listening," I said.

"Growing up, this bitch named Tameka Fletcher tortured me from junior high into high school, telling all the kids I was a lesbian just because I was really into sports. She would hit me, tease me, and even got my other classmates to join in on her bullying. My teammates would shove me into lockers, call me all sorts of names, and humiliate me. I was so hurt by their words that I felt like there was something wrong with me. Even though sports were my life and made me happy, I wanted to quit altogether because the bullying killed the fun I had when I played. The girls who were lesbians on the sports teams I was on didn't want any more drama and attention than they already had, so they left me to fend for myself."

She appeared to be still pained by that memory.

"So, what happened?" I asked.

"I prayed to God every day—even when it felt like He wasn't listening, even when it felt like things would never get better. I believed in Him and knew He would help me. God works in mysterious ways. In my sophomore year, my body started to mature—"

"Yeah, it did," I said, interrupting her.

She playfully slapped my arm and continued. "My ex, Travis, asked me one day if I was really a lesbian. He was the captain of the boys' basketball team at the time, so all the girls wanted him. I immediately told him that I wasn't. He confessed to me that he always thought I was hot but never approached me because he thought I was into girls. We went on a few dates, and eventually, he asked me to be his girl. I wanted all the teasing to end. So, even though he wasn't my type, I said, yes. I truly believe God presented that opportunity. He gave Travis the courage that day to approach me, and once I agreed to be his girl, all the teasing stopped. I became popular and finished high school enjoying sports with no drama. Sammy, if you believe, God will present you with opportunities."

I nodded, not because I agreed but because I wanted to move on from the topic. I listened to her tell me more about Travis and high school.

"I don't know . . . Even during our best times, I've always felt like something was missing. I never felt totally happy or fulfilled with him. I don't know if it's because of his immaturity or his laziness, but there was always something off with us," Sasha stated.

I wanted to hear more about what she felt was missing. I wanted to see how hard I would have to work to hit that. Maybe what was lacking was desire and attraction.

"What do you think was missing? Were you not pleased sexually?" I asked, grinning to myself.

"No, it wasn't anything like that. He was decent in bed, but I never felt like our connection was strong. I never felt that 'spark' with him. I felt like I was only going through the motions in our relationship."

"Is he the only man you've been with?"

"No. I've been with three other guys besides him during our little breakups. I was tired of him fucking around on me, so I wanted to see what else was out there. Even with those guys, something was always missing."

"If you didn't feel a connection with him and you were tired of his shit, why are you so upset that it's finally over?"

"I don't know. It was a comfort thing. I've been with him for so long that he's all I know. Even with the other guys I've dealt with in between, there was nothing there. I felt like being with them was what I was supposed to do."

"You should do what you feel is right for you, not what you think you're supposed to do," I told her.

I let her vent more about her frustrations, and after a lot of drinking on both of our parts, we ended up falling asleep on my couch.

"You're right. She does have a pretty mouth. She has those nice full lips that I like," the white truck driver said while squeezing my left knee.

"See, I told you. Just give me fifty bucks, and she'll suck you real good . . . I promise," Joan told him.

"Can I have a bareback blow job?"

"No, daddy, she has to suck you with a condom on."

"What if I say no deal unless it's bareback?"

"Come on. You should be glad I only have her suck men with a condom on. This way, you know her young mouth is clean."

"You got a point there."

I sat in the front cabin of a Mack truck with my mother and this random truck driver as they discussed me

*sucking him off as if I weren't there. Tears rolled down my
cheeks as he handed my mother money so her 12-year-
old child could suck his dick. My mother was unmoved
by my crying. I already knew I would be providing this
service at least six or seven more times before the night
was over.*

*The truck driver unzipped his blue jeans and pulled
out his small, uncircumcised cock. He rolled on a condom. I didn't want to look at him. I snuck subtle glances
of his erection from the corner of my eye. I was tired of
this shit every night. I prayed to God every day, but nothing ever changed.*

*My mother grabbed me by the back of my head and
tried to lower me down to his lap, but I stiffened my neck
and resisted.*

*"Sammy, put him in your mouth right now," Joan
instructed me. "Stop playing around."*

*I shook my head and ignored her. I kept my eyes
straight, staring out the big windshield of the truck. The
truck driver started to get impatient. He put his thick,
pudgy hands on the nape of my neck and shoved me
forward.*

"Come on, little darling, do as you're told."

*I stiffened up, even more, cringing at his touch. I
continued not to look at him. My mother backhanded
slapped me.*

*"Do you want to fucking eat tonight or not? Suck him
now, or I swear you won't eat shit for the rest of the
week," she threatened.*

*I was starving already. I knew my mother wasn't bull-
shitting with her threat. She strong-armed me into doing
shit often by taking away my food. While other children
enjoyed treats like cheeseburgers from McDonald's and*

Burger King or a frosty from Wendy's, I was left to eat
peanut butter and jelly sandwiches in our low-income,
run-down apartment.

The truck driver's grip got stronger on my neck. "Open
your mouth, bitch," he commanded. He lowered me down
to his dick. My mouth opened . . .

I woke up screaming, jerked from my nightmarish
past, and back to my mediocre present. I covered my
mouth to muffle the sounds as I shook and breathed heavily. Beads of sweat dripped down my forehead. I wrapped
my arms around myself and began rocking to calm down.

Quickly, I ran to the bathroom, turned on the faucet,
cupping my hand under the cold, running water, and
splashed it on my face. I cupped it again and slowly
brought the water up to my mouth to drink it out of my
hands. That nightmare made me remember the horrible
aftertaste of lube and sweat that I had in my mouth from
giving head back then.

Sasha was still sound asleep on the couch. I was
jittery, but I forced myself to walk to my linen closet to
get an extra blanket and pillow for her. I placed the pillow
under her head and covered her with the blanket. She
stirred; her eyes opened slightly. She smiled at me and
went back to sleep.

Sasha woke up around 8:00 a.m. She stretched and
yawned, then jumped when she realized she had slept
at my place on my couch. She quickly checked to make
sure all of her clothes were on. I smiled to myself.

"I'm so sorry I spent the night drooling all over your
couch. Those drinks hit me hard," she said.

I laughed. "I enjoyed your company."

I made breakfast. While we ate, I joked about her snoring. Sasha spoke with such diction and passion. The girl could talk, but it was cute. I liked seeing her open up and being comfortable. Slowly but surely, she was becoming more at ease with me. She even asked if she could sleep over again sometime. I licked my lips at the thought of turning her out.

Five

Pain Is Love

I drove home after dropping Sasha at the club to pick up her car. While listening to Z100, Katy Perry's "E.T." came on. I laughed to myself because she has so many songs that make me think she's a closet lesbian. The first verse and chorus to that song reminded me of Cheryl, the woman who opened my eyes.

Usually, because the court system was so backed up with bigger crimes, prostitution was treated with a slap on the wrist. I usually made a plea with the district attorney to drop my crime to a lesser charge, got forced to do some bullshit counseling that I never got anything out of, maybe did a few community service hours, and the whole process was like a revolving door. After being pinched for prostitution numerous times, the judge finally had enough of my shit. He didn't allow a plea deal, nor did he lessen my charges. This time around, he hammered me because of all my repeat offenses, and I was sentenced to do a two-year bid at the Albion Correctional Facility in Albion, New York.

While doing my time, I crossed paths with a woman named Cheryl. She changed my philosophy on relationships and life in general.

I had been in holding cells in precincts, been held at central booking, I even did short stints of time on Rikers Island, but this was my first time in an actual prison, so I didn't know what to expect. I was scared, but I walked with confidence and hardened my face. I didn't want to show an ounce of weakness. I followed closely behind the muscular corrections officer walking me to my new cell. His thick mustache and dark, slicked-back black hair reminded me of one of the johns who used to rape me as a kid, which made a chill run through me.

My arms were weighed down by the extra regulation uniforms I was given. Women had their faces pressed against the bars in an attempt to get a glimpse of the new "fresh fish." They heckled me and made nasty comments as we passed by numerous cells on the way to mine.

"Oooh, come here new pussy," a random female voice called out.

"I smell new fish," a raspy-voiced female said through her cell as she blew me a kiss.

I cringed at their catcalling. Feelings of anxiety and fear made my heart feel like it would beat out of my chest.

"Keep moving, inmate," the correction officer said.

Ignoring the other inmates' tongue flickering and pointing, I kept my eyes fixed on the back of the correction officer and focused on reaching my cell.

"You're a pretty one. I'll be watching you," the white corrections officer said, slapping me on the ass. His badge displayed the name "Johnson."

I didn't like his comment or him touching me like that, but I kept my mouth shut as we walked. We stopped in front of one of the cells.

"Open cell D-24," Johnson yelled out.

The large steel cell doors opened. A beautiful woman was on the top bunk reading a magazine. She wore the same bright orange jumpsuit I was wearing.

"I'll let you two ladies get acquainted. Cheryl, you're going to like this one. She's a real looker." He laughed and slapped me on the ass again. "Y'all play nice now." He blew a kiss at me.

Once I walked into the cell, the resounding sound of the steel door closing behind me caused me to jump and solidified in my mind that this was real. That sound made it feel so final. I was trapped in the eight-by-eight-foot cement tomb. The cell was filthy. Dust and dirt covered the floor, and remnants of dead bugs were scattered all over. A stainless-steel toilet with no toilet seat and a clogged sink with murky water in it stood in the corner. There were no mirrors, only a small four-inch piece of shiny aluminum that could be used to see your blurred reflection. I looked at my bed. There wasn't even a pillow or blanket on it, just a thin white sheet. I felt like I had landed straight into hell.

Cheryl jumped down off her bed and looked me up and down. I'm tall for a woman, but next to her six-foot-one-inch frame, she made me look small. Her silky jet-black hair was pulled into a ponytail, and she looked rugged. The words "Pain Is Love" were tattooed on her neck.

"That bastard was right. You are beautiful," Cheryl said.

"Thanks," I replied softly.

"Is this your first time here?"

"Yeah."

"This place will show you who you really are. If you don't figure things out the first time, you'll keep coming here until you do. The bottom bunk is yours. As long as you don't touch my shit, we should get along fine."

"Have you been here before?" I asked.

"Yep."

She was pretty, which surprised me. I figured inmates were rough and hideous, but she wasn't. Her eyebrows were done to perfection, and her prison jumper hugged her curves to a tee. Her smooth, dark cocoa skin complemented her silky, jet-black hair.

While she was being cordial with me, I kept my guard up. I knew I was gay, but I hadn't slept with a woman yet. It is one thing to experience your first time with someone you're willing to share it with; it's another to have your first time taken by force. I had my virginity taken by a man and loathed it. I wanted my first experience with a woman to be memorable, and with someone I truly loved and gave my heart to. I didn't want my first time with a woman to be tainted the same way it was with men.

Cheryl circled me. I balled up my fist, ready to swing if she tried to start some shit.

"Relax, li'l mama. I'm not going to fuck with you," she whispered in my ear.

She grabbed the wobbly iron rails of the bunk and lifted herself back on top. I sat on the bottom cot, listening to the creaks above me as she moved around to get comfortable. I tried to make conversation to ease the tension.

"What are you in for?" I asked.

"Li'l mama, didn't anyone tell you that you're not supposed to ask questions like that when you're in here?"

"Sorry."

There was an awkward silence for a moment.

"What are you in here for?" Cheryl asked.

I hesitated to tell her. "Trickin'. What about you?"

"Drugs. Do you have a man on the outside?"

I didn't know if I should answer that. I worried if I said no, she would try something.

I braced myself and answered, "No. Do you?"

She laughed at my question. "Li'l mama, I'm not into men."

"Oh," I said, my voice wavering.

"Calm down. I'm not going to touch your goodies . . . at least not tonight anyway."

I felt somewhat comfortable, but I had no idea what would be in store for me in that place.

"Bitch, what the fuck are you looking at?" a light-skinned black woman with cornrows asked a blond-haired white woman.

I was sitting alone in the cafeteria. Cheryl was sitting at a table across from me with five other women, unaffected by the scuffle near us.

"Not much, bitch," the blonde responded.

The woman with cornrows stood up and stepped to the blonde. "Eye problems? You wanna do something?" Cornrows asked.

"Settle down, inmates," a female guard said, stepping closer to them.

The blond woman dug in her pocket. It looked like she was holding something as she punched Cornrows in the stomach. Cornrows was bleeding and immediately began strangling the blonde. The blonde dropped a sharp piece of metal on the floor next to my foot that she had hidden in her grip. I quickly and discreetly picked it up and put it in my pocket for protection.

I didn't get any sleep the first week. Between women testing me at mealtime and in the yard, I stayed getting

*into fights. At night, I guarded myself in case Cheryl
tried to touch me at lights out, but luckily, she didn't try
anything. I should have been more concerned about the
guards. They would often enter my cell in the middle of
the night and take turns having their way with me. I tried
my hardest not to make a peep when they fucked me, but
they would be purposely rough.*

"Yeah, take this dick," Johnson said in my ear.

*I winced as his nasty cock penetrated me forcefully
from behind.*

*"Ugh . . . That's some sweet pussy you got there. Keep
it tight for me, okay, baby?" Johnson laughed as he fixed
his uniform.*

*"And you, Cheryl. You didn't see shit. If I hear you
even whispered it to God, you and your crew of dykes are
finished. Do you understand?" Johnson asked.*

*"I don't know what you're talking about, boss. What
is it that I was supposed to have seen?" Cheryl said
casually.*

"Exactly . . ."

*The guards laughed. They left me naked, facedown on
my cot. I was sore and hurt in every way imaginable. I
tried to be strong and chalk it up to being a routine of
having men fuck me literally and figuratively, but the
pain from my past and the experiences in that hellhole
became too overwhelming. I sobbed uncontrollably into
my cot to muffle the noise. Soon, I reached under my
mattress and pulled out the small shard of metal that I
had been secretly sharpening. I had been contemplating
ending things for a while. I held the blade against my
wrist. My hands trembled. I wanted the pain to stop. I
wanted my shitty existence to end. As I pressed the blade
firmly against my skin, I heard Cheryl hop off her cot.*

"Don't do it. Give that to me," she said softly.

My hands and lips trembled. Cheryl held me, and I slowly dropped the metal. She consoled me by rubbing my back.

"Shhh, li'l mama. Everything is going to be okay," she said.

"I . . . I . . . can't take this shit anymore. All men ever want from me is to fuck me. I'm so tired of my fucked-up life. I just want it all to stop. I should end this shit and put myself out of my fucking misery."

"That's not the answer. You're hurting right now, but things will get better. You have to find something that makes you feel good. You need a positive release. Killing yourself is just the easy way out."

"That's easy for you to say. They're not fucking you in every hole in your body."

"Who do you think they were fucking before you got here? They did the same thing to me. Then you came around. Now you're the fresh meat. Eventually, someone else will come here that catches their eye, and they'll go after them."

She listened to me gripe. What I really liked about her was that she was so attentive. She never talked over me. I felt like she was genuinely listening to me instead of waiting for her turn to talk. That night, I lay there looking up at the metal bed frame above me. Even though I hadn't completely grown to trust her yet, I was happy to be cell mates with her.

Our bond grew as the days passed, and Cheryl and I became inseparable. She became my best friend. She was the only person I confided in while I was locked up. I told her things I had never told another soul. I shared my whole fucked-up childhood and my struggles growing up in the foster care system with her. She told me about being betrayed by her male childhood best friend who let her take the fall for drug possession. She would listen to me read the letters that Silka and Jaime sent, and she was my protection when other female inmates tried to test me. I remember when she helped me when I was attacked one day in the shower.

"What's up, new booty?" a white, dirty-blond-haired woman asked.

I was in the shower, trying my best to hurry up and get out of there before more women came. I wrapped my large beige terry cloth towel around my naked body, gathered my clothes, and attempted to leave.

"Nothing. I was just leaving," I replied.

Out of nowhere, the white woman's four friends surrounded me. My panic-stricken eyes darted around the room. She stroked my face and ran her fingers through my untamed hair. I moved away, but I was bumped back toward her by one of her friends.

"Where do you think you're going? Did I give you permission to leave? You didn't pay your toll yet. I'm Vicki. I run shit here, and what I want . . . I get," she said.

She reached for my towel. I tried to pry her fingers off, but her grip was too strong. She yanked my towel from my body in one swift motion, leaving me naked. Her friends laughed at my embarrassment. There was no way in hell that I was going to go out without a fight. So I stepped to her, balled up my fist, and swung at her face with all my might. One of her friends caught my arm before it reached her.

"Face me without your goons, you bitc—"

Before I could finish my sentence, Vicki was on me. She punched me in the face, grabbed me by my hair, and slammed me against the tile wall. The impact of my skull colliding against the wall made me clutch the back of my head and slide down to the floor.

"You two, watch the doors. You guys hold her down," Vicki instructed.

Vicki yanked me by my feet. My back slid on the slippery wet shower floor. She mounted me while one woman held my feet, and the other held my arms. Vicki ran her fingers from my breast, down to my stomach, and traced her fingers around my folds.

"Get off me, you bitch!" I screamed.

"If you're not going to give it to me, I'll just have to take it," Vicki said.

She wrapped her thighs around my hips. Her left hand gripped my throat, and she placed her other hand over my mouth. I shook my head intensely to try to get her hand off my mouth.

"Bitch, you better not scream or I'll end you," Vicki threatened.

Vicki licked the side of my face. She reached down toward my vagina again. I jerked my body roughly, trying to fight her off me, but her friends held me down tightly. It was no use. Then she punched me in the face.

"Stop fucking squirming!"

My face stung like I had been hit with a brick. I turned my head, ready to get raped again. I didn't want to see her eyes. I didn't want to remember the expression on her face when she fucked me. Suddenly, I heard voices at the door and the commotion of fighting.

"What the fuck do you think you're doing? She's mine. I claimed her already, and you know that, Vicki," Cheryl said.

When I heard her voice, I turned my head excitedly. Cheryl and her group of five friends were in the shower sporting intimidating faces. I didn't know if I should be happy that she was there or scared by her comment.

"I don't know shit. That's news to me," Vicki said.

"Well, if you didn't know, you know now. I already claimed her, so get off her, or we're gonna have a problem," Cheryl replied.

Vicki sucked her teeth and motioned for her friends to release me.

"Next time, let it be known when you claim one of the new fishies, so there's no confusion," Vicki responded angrily.

Vicki purposely shoulder bumped Cheryl as she and her group of flunkies walked out. After she and her friends left, Cheryl helped pick me up off the wet floor.

"Thanks—"

"Don't . . . Don't thank me. Don't say shit; just get dressed," Cheryl said angrily.

I nodded, thanked her friends, and did as I was told.

Cheryl was the voice of reason during the times when I felt suicidal. My attraction to her grew daily. I didn't worry about her trying to fuck me while I was asleep; I welcomed it. Our first sexual experience felt like my first time making love.

"I'm cold. Do you mind if I cuddle with you to keep warm?" Cheryl asked as she climbed onto my cot.

"Not at all. I'd love to cuddle with you," I said.

Cheryl wrapped her arm around me from behind and pulled me close. I felt her warm breath on the nape of my neck. Her dainty fingertips grazed up and down my spine, pausing only to switch to rubbing the small of my back. I closed my eyes. I felt completely relaxed and uninhibited by her touch. I arched my back, pushing my ass into her crotch. She gradually made her way from lightly strok-ing my back to cupping my breasts and gently kissing the side of my face.

Before I knew it, I was completely naked with my back still facing her. Cheryl wiggled her middle and ring finger, parted my lips, and entered my moist vagina. She pushed her fingers in and out repetitively, which drove me wild. Then she nibbled on my earlobe.

"Does that feel good?" she asked.

I nodded. Her voice vibrated in my ear, sending a tingle down my spine. I was lost in the sensation. Cheryl quickly turned me over on my back. She placed her hands on the sides of my face and kissed me deeply. She placed light kisses all over my nipples and ran her tongue over the middle of my breasts. She reinserted her fingers. She held my left nipple firmly with her lips, gently tugging on it. The base of her palm rubbed vigorously against my clit, stimulating me to the point of sensory overload. Before I knew it, my vagina started to flutter uncontrollably. My muscles began to spasm steadily. It felt like electricity was coursing through every cell in my body as I came for the first time. I jerked at the tingling that ran through me.

Cheryl positioned herself so that her face was directly against my vagina. She soothingly blew warm air on my sensitive clit. Her tongue was long and thick; my hips moved upward to meet it with every lick. She sucked on the head of my clit, causing me to moan loudly. I rocked forward, grinding my pelvis in her face as she devoured my flower. It wasn't long until that feeling of electricity hit me again. Cheryl maneuvered herself against me into a scissor position. The feeling of her vagina pressed firmly against mine intensified my arousal. Cheryl's grinding, rubbing, and hard thrusting of her hips against my wetness caused my pussy to throb. Feeling our juices intermingling brought me to orgasm again.

Afterward, I was exhausted. Cheryl gently caressed my face as I lay comfortably nestled in her arms. She lulled me into a much-needed peaceful sleep.

Months went by. Finally, I was a month away from being released. As far as intimacy went, sex with Cheryl became more intense as she explained to me what she liked. I learned more about her body and became more experienced. While that aspect was great, I felt things were changing emotionally. She became distant. I noticed that she and her friends would often ignore and try to avoid me. One day I confronted her about it.

"So, I'm getting out next month. I'll write to you every week until you get out. Then we can try to find a place together," I said enthusiastically.

Cheryl lay on her cot with her legs crossed as she read a book. She shook her head and laughed to herself.

"I don't know if that's a good idea, li'l mama," she said.

I didn't know it then, but this conversation would become my new philosophy for relationships in the future.

"Why is that?" I asked, sounding disappointed.

"Because when we get out of here, we're both going to return to our own worlds."

I frowned at her choice of words. "I don't get it. What exactly are you saying? Are you saying you don't want to have anything to do with me once we're out of here?"

"I don't want to sound like a bitch, but no, I don't. We're all in a fucked-up place here. To make that time go by easier, we have to try to make the best out of things. Do you know what Slim Fast is?"

I looked at her like she had three fucking heads. What the fuck did our relationship have to do with Slim Fast?

"It's a fucking diet drink. What does that have to do with us?"

"Slim Fast is a meal replacement. It's used as a substitute for food. While it might not be the nice juicy steak dinner we want, it has enough to sustain us and suppress our hunger."

"What's your point?"

"My point is, there is no me and you. You were merely something to make my time here easier. You were enough to keep me satisfied while I was in this hellhole, but when you're gone, that's the end of it."

At that moment, I hated Cheryl. I had trusted her. I cared for her. I fell in love with her, and she treated my feelings and the time we spent together like it was just an emotional snack. I cried hysterically. She continued to lay there with an impassive expression.

"Did everything between us mean nothing to you?" I asked.

"Honestly, no. You served your purpose, and I served mine. I knew as soon as you walked into this cell that I could easily turn you out. You were already gay, so it made seducing you easier. If you take someone by force, it can be enjoyable because you have that sense of power over them, but if you can get someone to do what you want willingly, that's real power. I never forced you to do anything. You made your own decisions."

Angered and hurt, I grabbed her leg, attempting to pull her off the cot. She quickly jabbed me in the face, sending me stumbling backward. I fell to the floor. Cheryl hopped down and stood over me. My nose was bleeding.

"I fucking hate you!" I yelled. I spat at her. She wiped her face. I thought she would hit me again, but she just looked at me like I was pitiful.

"Do you really? Let's think about that for a moment. When you needed to vent, I listened. When you felt like shit, I made you feel special. When you had your little nightmares, I helped you through them. When you felt like ending your pathetic little life, I gave you a reason to live. You don't hate me. Before you met me, you were a confused little girl who didn't know who or what she was. Think about it now. Do you know who you are?"

I sat on the floor thinking about everything she said.

"I might not have been what you wanted, but at this point in your life, I'm what you needed. I set you free. That's my parting gift to you," she continued.

"And you feel good about that?"

"Actually, I do. I've had a major impact on your life. It's because of me that you're not a confused little bitch on the fence trying to figure out if you're gay, straight, or bi. No matter how much you hate me or how angry you are, I'm immortalized in your memory. Everyone can't say they'll be remembered in a person's life like that."

Cheryl hopped back on her cot and returned to reading as if nothing happened. Our friendship—or whatever we had—ended that day. I lay on my cot and quietly cried myself to sleep.

During my last couple of weeks, we barely spoke.

She was right. When I was released from Albion Correctional Facility, I never heard from or saw her again. She went on with her life, and I moved on with mine. At the time, I was hurt. I hated her, but as time went on, I understood the method to her madness. I often reflected on everything that happened between us. I wanted the freedom she experienced. She used me, and even though I hated her for that, she helped me become who I am. People like Cheryl couldn't be hurt because they wouldn't allow themselves to get hurt. I needed to be like her. I wanted to be like Cheryl—to be unscathed by life's bullshit. When I was released from prison, I came home a different person. Being in the streets and foster homes taught me how to fight, but being incarcerated taught me how to survive.

I had served my time and was finally being released.

"Oh my God! It's so good to have you back, girl, finally," Silka said.

Silka, Jaime, and Dom, who I would soon get to know, greeted me at the release gate. I scrunched up my face at the sight of him.

"Who's the dude? You never mentioned any guys in your letters," I said.

"This is Dom, my boyfriend. I've told him everything about you. He couldn't wait to meet you."

"I wish I could say the same."

Everyone laughed except me.

"Where do you want to go first now that you're a free woman?" Jaime asked.

"I want to get a tattoo. I learned something while being locked up in there that I don't ever want to forget."

"Cool. It's our treat. We got you. Let's get you out here."

I smiled at my friends. I missed and loved them.

I walked into my apartment and stopped reflecting on the past. I took a shower, then called Virginia to see if she could sneak away for an early-morning romp. I guess you could say my inner Cheryl was surfacing.

Six

Seduction

Sasha was lonely and broken. Her vulnerability made it easy for me to work my magic and gain her trust. Since she was a so-called straight, I wanted to bring her into my world gradually without scaring her off so she wouldn't feel grossed out with being with a woman sexually. She was going to be a challenge, but she would be just another conquest I added to my bedpost.

For the most part, Sasha stayed to herself and had few friends. So I decided to invite her out with my friends. Although Silka and Jaime were straight, they hung out with me at gay bars all the time. Seeing them comfortable would undoubtedly help Sasha feel at ease. While I acted friendly with her, I didn't want to be stuck in the friendship zone. I flirted with her often and openly expressed that I would love to date her one day.

It was a Friday, and as we drove to Silka's house, I could tell Sasha was uncomfortable. She was fidgety and kept wringing her hands. I found her uneasiness to be cute.

"Don't sweat it. These girls are my family. If I like hanging out with you, I know they will too," I told her.

Silka and Jaime had been around girls I was trying to court before, so they knew the routine.

We pulled up to Silka's house. Dom opened the door seconds after I rang the bell.

"Well well well . . . If it isn't my least favorite white boy," I said.

"Aaaw, you know you love me." Dom pinched my cheek.

I knocked his hand away; then Sasha and I walked in.

"Keep your dirty little sausages off me, loser," I said.

"I love you too, Samantha." Dom turned to Sasha. "Hi, I'm Dominic, Silka's husband."

"Hi, I'm Sasha."

"It's nice to meet you, Sasha."

I didn't like the way he was gawking at her.

"I know you're not flirting with Sasha in front of me. I'm just waiting to catch you slippin', and when you do, I'ma fuck you up."

Silka yelled from the kitchen, "Sam, please don't threaten to beat up my husband!"

I rolled my eyes at Dom. "I'll try my best. Just making sure he knows to come correct."

Jaime walked out of the kitchen.

"Pay them no mind. This is how they always act," Jaime said.

"Hey, Jaime," Sasha said excitedly.

They hugged and exchanged pleasantries while Dom tried to make small talk with me.

"So where are you taking my lovely wife tonight?" he asked.

"Ooh, are we going to Henrietta Hudson?" Jaime asked.

"Hell no!"

Jaime sucked her teeth and whined, "Why?"

"I always have to check my hat when we go in there. Plus, it's filled with new lezzes and baby dykes. I don't feel like dealing with the teenyboppers when I'm not hunting."

Jaime looked at me; then her eyes darted off to Sasha. We communicated with our looks. Her eyes asked what the hell I was thinking by saying "hunting." While my statement was bold, I wasn't worried. This whole situation was new to Sasha, and my comment seemed to go over her head.

I shrugged.

"Also, they always cater to the light-skinned Hispanics and *his* kind." I pointed to Dom. "We're going to Ginger's in Brooklyn."

"Is that another lesbian bar? Why are you always taking your friends to gay places?" Dom asked.

"Not that it's any of your business, but my friends go with me to these places because they're fun, and they know I'm more comfortable there. When I go to straight bars and clubs, dirty-ass men hit on me. I end up feeling out of place and awkward."

"Kind of like being the only white guy in a hip-hop club," he said, attempting to make a joke.

"Like a typical man, you have to make it all about you," I said.

"I was just trying to say I know what that feels like."

"White man, it's your world. How could you ever feel out of place? Look at you. A white man that's still stealing black women."

"Samantha, stop picking on my husband!" Silka yelled again from the kitchen.

Dom laughed and shook his head. "It's okay, babe. Sam, am I still your least favorite white boy?"

"Always," I replied.

Sasha nudged me.

"Why are you so mean to him? You should show him at least some kind of respect in his house."

"Why? He ain't nobody. I'm not a fan of men, and I'm an even lesser fan of white men."

"Don't sweat it, Sasha. Sam and I have a love-hate relationship. She loves to hate me," he said jokingly.

I gave him the finger. Silka came out of the kitchen.

"Always a pleasure, Sam," he said, then kissed Silka. "Have fun, baby. I love you."

"I love you too, babe. Dinner is in the oven. It should be ready in forty-five minutes. Don't leave it in any longer than that.

"I left the food for the baby in the fridge, so everything is set." Dom nodded and waved her away. Silka faced us.

"Y'all ready to go? Where we headed?" Silka said.

"Sam wants to hang out at Ginger's," Jaime told her.

"I don't care where we go as long as I can get a good buzz. All week, the kids in my class have been driving me nuts."

I drove us to Park Slope in Brooklyn. We walked into Ginger's laughing at all the questions Sasha had about going to lesbian bars.

"So, are all the lesbians . . . I mean women at the bar, going to be manly?" she asked.

I laughed. "I'm a lesbian. Do I come across as manly to you?"

"No, you're feminine, but you flirt with me just as hard as any man has."

We all laughed at that.

The bar had a long wooden counter, tan stools, and a pool table in the back. At first glance, you'd think it was just a typical bar, but the laid-back atmosphere, seeing women running the place and having a good time, made this place fun for me.

As soon as we walked in, all eyes were on us. Our group had the attention of every stud, AG (aggressive girl), femme, and butch in the place. A stud sporting a Mohawk and lip ring approached us. Her eyes were as black as her skin. The only thing light about her was her pearly white teeth.

"How are you ladies doing? The name's Pat."

"We're good, Pat. Thanks," I said, then turned my head to show we weren't interested.

She walked up to Sasha and grabbed her hand. "You look really good tonight. Can I buy you a drink?"

I pulled Sasha close and said, "She's with me."

"She's got a mouth, right? If she didn't want me talking to her, she'd say something, right?"

"*I'm* saying something. Back off!"

I stared her down, sizing her up. She was about five foot eleven with a muscular build.

"My bad, sis. Sorry about that. Are they all 'family'?" Pat asked, indirectly inquiring if all of my friends were lesbians.

"Nah, just me. They're just visiting," I said.

"Oh, all right. Well, y'all have a good night," she said.

She headed back to her group, but I kept my eyes open for her. I knew how studs operated. They're abrasive, aggressive, and sometimes, they're pushier than men when they're trying to bed a woman.

We got to Ginger's early for happy hour. Silka put us on the waiting list to play pool while I found us seats on the spacious, cozy patio. We nursed our drinks and had food delivered from Belleville Bistro. Jaime told us fun gossip about her new job, while Sasha and I told stories of some of the funny experiences we had at the strip club.

"Ugh! Can you not smoke that cancer stick around me?" Sasha asked.

"Yeah . . . Ever since I had Georgia, cigarette smoke makes me nauseated. Put that out," Silka said.

"You act like you didn't use to smoke," I said.

"The key words are 'used to.' I only started doing it back in the day because you and Jaime did it."

"Being broke helped me to quit. It was either buy cigarettes or eat, and my big ass needs to eat," Jaime said.

We snickered at her comment.

I took a long drag of my cigarette and flicked it away. "You guys are a pain in my ass."

We left the patio area and went inside the bar. DJ Crissy P. was spinning records. "Milkshake," by Kelis came on.

"This used to be my shit back in the day," Jaime said as she rallied all of us to the dance floor.

Sasha's small waist and tight ass looked good in her black mini skirt. It gave me a nice view of her shapely, toned legs. She and Jaime swayed their hips seductively to the beat, while Silka and I danced modestly together. Before I knew it, the stud from earlier was pushing up on Sasha again.

"Back the fuck off. I told you that she's with me," I yelled.

She shoved me. Her breath reeked of liquor. "Who the fuck do you think you're screaming at? Get the fuck out of my face, bitch," she said angrily.

Pat grabbed Sasha, who tried to wiggle out of her grip and pushed her face away to block Pat from kissing her on the mouth. Pat was unrelenting and wouldn't let Sasha go. I pried her hands off of Sasha and shoved her back.

"Hey, hey! Cut that shit out! If you ladies want to fight, take that shit outside. We don't put up with that in here," the bartender shouted.

One of Pat's friends walked up to her. "Yo, fuck this. Let's bounce. Catty Shack is better than this slum anyway."

Pat nodded. We stared each other down while she got her coat. I stayed on guard until I saw her leave. Sasha looked a little uneasy. She rubbed the sides of her arms and wouldn't take her eyes off the floor. Silka noticed her demeanor.

"All right, ladies, the pool tables are open for us," Silka said.

"Don't let that shit ruin your night. Come on so I can bust your ass in pool," I said.

"You must've had too much to drink because there is no way you're beating me. I've been playing since I could walk. Growing up, we had a pool table in the basement."

Jaime and Silka turned their heads to conceal their laughter.

They knew I was talking shit to lay down game.

"Why don't we play for something?" I asked her.

"I don't know . . . Play for what?" Sasha asked skeptically.

"I'll play you for kisses, and none of that peck shit either. I'm talking tongue and everything," I laughed.

"Nah, I can't do that."

"Ah, come on. You were so confident just a minute ago. If you're that good, you don't even have to worry about kissing me."

"That is true, but what do I get when you lose?"

"For every game, you win, I'll give you twenty bucks."

"Oh, bet! And my rent is coming up too. You're going *down*," Sasha laughed as she racked the balls on the table.

I let her break. By the skin of my teeth, I won the first game.

"All right now, a deal is a deal. It's time to pucker up," I said.

"I'm not kissing you. Besides, your breath probably reeks of cigarettes."

"I'd quit tonight if you swear you'll kiss me."

"I don't know. I don't want to give women in here the wrong idea."

"Everyone here isn't worried about us. Besides, it's just a kiss."

"Maybe if your breath didn't smell like cigarettes . . ."

I ran to the bar and grabbed a handful of mints. Sasha laughed at my action.

"A bet is a bet. Don't renege on our agreement."

"If you swear you'll quit smoking tonight, I'll kiss you."

"Cross my fucking heart."

Sasha stepped close to me. I licked my lips. My gaze was constant and firm. I raised my hand, touched her soft face, and drew her in for the kiss. At first, it felt awkward, but as it went on, it felt natural. I savored all of her flavors, caressing her tongue with mine. I eased myself away. Her mouth was still open, but her eyes remained closed.

"Wow," she whispered when she finally opened them slowly.

If she was sprung off a kiss, she hadn't experienced anything yet.

***

"Look at that!" Sasha said excitedly.

We stood on Christopher Street and watched the Pride parade. A float passed by with gay superheroes. Sasha loved it. She took pictures of everything she found interesting. We maneuvered through the massive crowd to get closer to the route.

"This crowd gets rough. Hold on to me, so we don't get separated," I said.

Sasha held my hand; she was so at ease with it. She trusted me, and I liked that.

While I loved Pride Week, sometimes it got to be a little too much. At times, it all seemed like a circus act, and our community was going way overboard. While the week had its quirks, I love what it represented. Every race, age, and social class was out representing—proud to be gay. I wanted Sasha to realize that it didn't matter if someone was in love with someone of the same sex—love is love. I wanted her to see the beauty in our relationships and the strength we screamed to the world. I wanted her to see that Pride was an event where everyone was free to be themselves.

"There are so many people out here. Is this your favorite time of the year?" Sasha asked.

"I love Pride Week, but we don't need a week or a parade to get dressed up and celebrate who we are. We should be happy to be who we are every day, not once a year for a weeklong party."

"This is so cool."

"Yeah. One day you have to come with me to Atlanta Pride and SweetHeat in Miami. It's nonstop partying."

"Hell yeah! I'm down for that."

Sasha turned to the woman next to us. "Excuse me. Can you take a picture of my friend and me?"

The woman smiled and said, "Of course, sis."

Sasha handed her camera to the woman. We hugged each other and smiled genuinely for the picture. She took a bunch of shots of us like we were doing a mini photo shoot.

"These pictures are beautiful. They're everything, y'all," the woman expressed.

We laughed and thanked her.

"This one is my favorite," Sasha said when she finished skimming through the pictures.

I had to admit it was my favorite too. We had our arms around each other's shoulders, and the smiles on our faces were so genuine. We looked so happy together—so proud. I loved it.

"When we get back to your place, can you print this one out so I can have a copy too?"

"Of course," I replied.

After we watched the parade, I took her to the Stonewall Inn, a gay club in Greenwich Village in Manhattan between Waverly and Fourth streets. I loved Stonewall because of its historical relevance. I smiled as Sasha rushed over to look at the pictures and glance over the articles that hung on the walls. I walked up to her.

"Shit wasn't good for gays in those days. Things have improved somewhat, but we still have a long way to go."

"I heard about the riots vaguely, but what actually happened?" she asked.

I liked that she was interested in learning about it. I told her the history of the Stonewall Riots and the Gay Liberation Movement. I shared the horrors that gays and lesbians faced in those times.

"Early in the morning on June 28th, 1969, the police raided the Stonewall Inn. Back then, it was common for the police to raid gay bars because it was illegal to be openly gay in a public place. On that day, that particular raid started a riot between the cops, the customers, and residents from the community. The cops roughly manhandled and beat up some of the employees and customers, throwing them out of the bar. The gay community decided they were tired of being beaten and treated like shit because of the cops' heavy-handedness. It led to six days of protests and violent bouts with the gay community outside of the bar, on adjoining streets, and in Christopher Park. Even though a lot of people got hurt fighting for the cause, the Stonewall Riots were the catalyst needed to spark a change for the gay rights movement in this country and around the world."

The empathy on her face as she listened intently to every word made me happy. I felt like she understood how Pride Week started in this place. Taking her to Pride Week was just the beginning. I introduced her to lesbian writers and poets like Anne Fleming, Audre Lorde, and Alice Walker. We watched movies that were pro-gay like *The Kids Are All Right, Bound,* and *Stranger Inside*.

I helped her study for school, and eventually, I hung out with her and her family regularly. Meeting her family for the first time was a memorable experience for me.

"What's wrong?" I asked.

She had been fidgety ever since I picked her up, tapping her feet and shifting in her seat.

"Okay . . . Please don't take this the wrong way, but can you do a few things for me before we get there?"

"What exactly is it you want me to do?" I asked.

"My parents are extremely religious. First, can you please avoid telling them that you're a lesbian?"

I didn't say I agreed, but I encouraged her to continue. "Go on."

"Can you please not tell them that I work at a strip club with you or that you're a stripper? I told them you work with me at a bar. I didn't tell my family which bar it was out of fear my brothers or sister would want to stop by."

Again, I didn't agree. "Is there anything else?"

"Can you please, please, please, not curse in front of them? You don't understand how religious my family is. Lastly, my parents are old school. Please, only call them Mr. and Mrs. Small. You can call my dad Reverend Small if you want. He likes that."

"Fuck, no!" I said jokingly, then laughed at the serious expression on her face.

"Please, Sam, I'm serious. You're my best friend. I want to be able to hang out with you and my family together."

I wasn't the type to hold my tongue or tame who I was, but since it was so important to her, I promised to try my best.

We parked in her parents' driveway. Her mother came out to greet us.

"How's my oldest baby doing?" Mrs. Small asked.

"I'm good, Mama. This is my friend Samantha."

When I reached to shake her hand, she pulled me in for a hug.

"Sasha's told me so much about you. You're the photographer, right?"

"That's me," I smiled.

"Well, come on in. I'll introduce you to the rest of the family."

We walked into the house where Sasha's family was sitting in the living room, shouting and yelling at the Giants game on TV. Their home was nice. They had a sixty-five-inch TV with a surround sound system that made me feel like I was at the stadium. They were all sitting comfortably on a huge black sectional sofa.

"Take your eyes off that idiot box for one second. Be respectful and introduce yourselves to Sasha's friend, Samantha," Mrs. Small said.

I shook everyone's hands as they introduced themselves. Both of Sasha's brothers were eye fucking the shit out of me. The men in her family shared the same masculine features—strong jawlines, broad shoulders, and muscular arms. Her sister, Josephine, looked like her dad, but there was no mistaking that Sasha was the spitting image of her mother. They shared the same milk chocolate complexion and chestnut eyes. In her day, you could tell she was fine.

"Damn, you look good as hell. You work with Sasha? I need to know where so I can show some support," Jimmy said.

"Don't you be cussing in this house, boy," Reverend Small told him firmly.

"Sorry, Dad. She looks so good, though. I couldn't help myself."

"Control your hormones, boy."

I held my tongue, gave a faux smile, and turned my head toward the football game.

"You watch football too?" Joseph asked me.

"Yep. I'm a die-hard Giants fan."

Joseph licked his lips and stared into my eyes.

"You and I need to go out. We have a lot in common. We're confident, sexy, and die-hard Giants fans," he said.

"I don't think that's a good idea. You're not really my type."

"Why? We have all those similarities and likes."

"More than you know," I replied with a giggle.

Sasha elbowed me in my side. I winked at her.

We spent the night at the dinner table stuffing our faces, talking about sports, and laughing about Sasha and her siblings' crazy times growing up.

"You're a great cook, Mrs. Small," I said.

"Thank you! The way these guys eat I'm glad there was some left for you," she responded jokingly.

"Do guys hit on my sister when she's bartending?" Joseph asked.

"Because we'll be right there on weekends to keep them in check," Jimmy added.

"Guys hit on her, but don't worry, I protect her," I told them.

Sasha discreetly nudged me again.

"I'm glad God sent you to look after our baby," Mrs. Small said.

"While I don't necessarily agree with her working there with all of those godless people, I appreciate you looking after her. Don't forget, Sasha, this job is only temporary until you finish school and get your real job," Reverend Small stated.

"I know, Dad." Sasha looked annoyed.

"We love you, baby. I know you might see it as us being controlling, but we're only trying to protect you. We're so proud of you. We only want to see you succeed and go far because we know God gave you the talent to do so," Mrs. Small added.

"I know, Mama. I love you guys too. I might not show it at times, but I appreciate all of your support."

While it was somewhat sappy, I loved that. I have to admit I was a little envious seeing all of the love and closeness they had as a family. They were so affectionate with each other—hugging, complimenting, telling each other "I love you," and joking around. They had so many happy memories as a family, while I couldn't remember one fond memory with mine. I replaced my family with surrogates like Silka and Jaime, but if I could change one thing about my life, I would want to have a real family that cared about me like Sasha's family did with her. I had heard that parents never admit to having a favorite child, but I could tell Sasha was their pride and joy by the look in their eyes when she spoke and the excitement in their voices when they shared her past accomplishments and embarrassing moments. Even though they did the same with all their children, they always spoke of Sasha first.

"I'm sorry. We've been talking about ourselves so much that we've been rude and hadn't let you talk. Please tell us about yourself, Samantha," Mrs. Small said.

Shit, I didn't know what to say, but the looks on their faces were so warm that I felt somewhat comfortable around them. Not wanting them to feel pity for me, I wasn't about to share my life story, so I decided I would tell them as little as possible.

"Uh, where should I start? I'm a photographer and a dance . . . um, bartender." I quickly caught myself slipping. Josephine looked at me suspiciously. "I'm trying to save up to open my own photography studio so I can one day quit working in that bar," I added.

"That's great, sugar. Do your folks live around here?" Mrs. Small asked.

"Unfortunately, they died when I was a teenager."

"Sorry to hear that but know that you're a friend of Sasha's and can always look at us as your family," Mrs. Small said.

Sasha smiled at me. Her family voiced their agreement to that comment. I couldn't help but smile.

The house phone rang. Mrs. Small got up to answer it.

"Do you go to church often?" Reverend Small inquired.

I needed to give an answer that wouldn't embarrass Sasha and wouldn't turn this into a long drawn out conversation.

"I do, but not as often as I should," I replied.

"Well, you're always welcome to become a part of our congregation."

Mrs. Small came back to the table. "Honey, Mrs. Jenkins is on the phone. She said she's going through an urgent matter and needs to discuss something with you."

"Excuse me, Samantha. I have to attend to a matter with a member of our congregation."

Mrs. Small's face said everything. I saw she was uncomfortable with Reverend Small going off to another room to talk to that woman, but she took a deep breath, put on a faux smile, and returned to her lively self. While it was nice for Sasha's father to invite me to his church, all I could think about was the women Sasha told me he'd slept with there. That thought brought me back to reality and back to the truth that men can't be trusted.

"Mrs. Small, I have a question."

"Yes, chile, what is it?"

"All of your children, except Sasha, have names that start with the letter *J*. Why is that?"

"When I was giving birth to her, I was having a lot of complications in the delivery room. Things were looking grim, and if she came out alive, it would've been considered a miracle. One of the black nurses in the room told me to pray. She held my hand, looked me in my eyes, and told me everything would be okay. She told me that God would give her the strength to help deliver this baby into the world. Her words were what I needed and uplifted my faith. I asked her what her name was so I could never forget it. She told me it was Sasha. I felt it was a sign from God that I name my child after her. Like that woman, I had faith that Sasha would make miracles happen in the world."

I nodded, envious of the loving and proud way Mrs. Small looked at Sasha.

"It was nice meeting you. You girls come back to visit us again soon, you hear?" Mrs. Small said.

"We will, Mama."

We waved goodbye and pulled off.

"Thank you," Sasha said.

"For what?"

"For being tactful. I know there were times when you wanted to say what you really felt, but you were nice and respectful to my family. I appreciate that."

"I only did it because I care about you."

I rested my hand on top of hers. She didn't move it. She didn't seem uncomfortable. I turned to look at her and was greeted by her smiling face.

"I know you do. I care about you too."

I felt that I was making significant progress. I met her family, she was becoming more comfortable with me every day, and she admitted that she cared about me. Her defenses were coming down.

We became joined at the hip. When we weren't together, we spent hours talking to each other on the phone.
When we weren't doing that, I missed her. I missed her
smile, her laugh, her scent, and the way she looked at
me with admiration. In some ways, I admired her. I felt
she was who I could've been if my childhood weren't so
fucked up. I had feelings for her that I've never had for
anyone else. I couldn't explain them and was baffled trying to figure out what specifically made me feel this way.
There wasn't just one reason I was drawn to her. I was
falling in love with everything she was. On top of these
feelings, I stopped smoking.

That was a big fucking deal for me.

Seven

Power

I pranced around in thigh-high black leather boots, with my tits spilling out of my red lace bra and my ass filling a pair of matching boy shorts. My shorts were so tight that I had to relax on the acrobatics on the pole out of fear of ripping them. I made my booty wave and clap, which drove the crowd wild.

Just when I seductively removed my boy shorts and dropped down into a right split, Mr. Smith and his buck-toothed driver, Tyrone, walked into the club. I looked for Virginia, but it was just the two of them. Mr. Smith's eyes stayed glued to me the entire time of my performance. He waved and motioned for me to come to him. I nodded. Once I finished my set, I started heading toward him, but some random guy stopped by. His eyes roamed all over my body.

"Excuse me, miss. I'm Lou, this is Will, and that's my boy, Chris, over there."

This cornball came up to me, pointing to his friends. The guy Chris looked like they had dragged him here against his will.

"My boy Chris is going through a bad divorce. I was wondering if you would like to come to the VIP room with us and cheer him up. You can bring two of your fine-ass friends too if you want. How much?"

I laughed at him. "Nigga, you can't afford this," I told him, then walked past him toward Mr. Smith.

"Fuck you, you stupid bitch!"

"Calm down, baby. I'll take you up on your offer," Cinnamon said. "Let me know what you're looking for, and I'll get some of my friends to join us."

Lou smiled. "Cool! See, we don't need your stank ass. Cinnamon got a bigger ass than you anyway," he called out from behind me.

Ignoring him, I put some pep in my step and continued to Mr. Smith's table. I took a seat on his lap and said, "Did you miss me, daddy? Are you two having a guys' night out or something?" I joked.

They didn't find my joke humorous.

"Mr. Smith would like you to join him in the VIP room— the same deal he made with you last time. Are you cool with that?" Tyrone asked.

I really didn't feel like having this fucker touch me. I dry heaved at the thought of feeling his sweaty paws on me, but I couldn't turn down an easy two grand. I would just have to shower and scrub myself thoroughly afterward.

I stood up from Mr. Smith's lap bent over in front of him and grabbed the back of my calves. I slowly shimmied up and faced him.

"Of course, we can do all the stuff he likes," I said as I winked at Mr. Smith.

Tyrone flashed a big grin, while Mr. Smith had a weird expression on his face. He slowly nodded while biting down on his bottom lip.

Tyrone headed for the room holding a briefcase as the bouncers looked him up and down. I found that odd, but I figured my money was in it, so I didn't care.

"Hand me my briefcase, Tyrone," Mr. Smith said. He reached in his khakis and handed Tyrone a thick roll of singles.

"Have fun. I'll see you soon," Mr. Smith said.

As soon as we walked into the room, Mr. Smith immediately got rough with me. He grabbed my arms firmly and shoved me to the floor. I wondered if this was how he acted when he was intimate with Virginia. I fell on my back. Mr. Smith pulled down his pants, rolled a condom on to his erection, and mounted me, placing his knees on each side of my head, so his dick was directly in my face.

"Suck it, bitch!" he commanded.

I did what he asked. Mr. Smith grabbed me by the hair and shoved his member down my throat. He thrusted his hips powerfully, jamming his shaft down my esophagus to the point where I was gagging and coughing. Despite all of that, I composed myself. I sucked him busily. I worked him in my mouth slurping and licking, figuring the faster I got him to come, the faster this shit would be over. He pulled his saliva-covered dick out of my mouth, picked me up, and placed me on the sofa.

"Get on all fours," he demanded, as he positioned me doggie style. I grabbed his cock and guided him into my opening. I rolled my eyes while facing away from him as he pounded me from behind. I was already beyond tired of his tough guy act. I prayed he would hurry up and come quickly so this rough shit could end. I was completely frustrated with the shit I had to endure just to make a couple of dollars, but I knew this was all temporary and for a greater purpose. Eventually, I'd have enough to open my studio, and this would all feel like a bad dream, like the rest of my shitty memories.

Mr. Smith stopped pumping into me. "Don't fucking move," he ordered.

I heard the briefcase open and felt lube being applied to my asshole. Mr. Smith wasn't long, but he was wide. I knew he would try to ram it in me so he could feel manly and powerful. As expected, he shoved his member into my asshole. I shrieked. He stroked me ruggedly. His knuckles dug into my scalp as he brought his face close to my right ear.

"You didn't think I would find out? You thought you two would keep fucking around behind my back, and I wouldn't know?"

I bit the cushions to keep myself from screaming. I needed more lube. The friction was killing me. I felt like he was going to rip my ass open. I released the pillow and grimaced from each thrust, but I didn't dare ask him to stop or beg for more lube. From my experience, asking for any type of mercy from men like him only excited them more and made things worse.

"What . . . What are you talking about?" I asked through gritted teeth, trying to play dumb.

"Don't fuck with me. I know that dyke bitch of a wife of mine sees you regularly. Once in a while when we come to dumps like this, it's fine, but when she tries to make this shit a regular occurrence and risk embarrassing my family name, I'm not fucking having it."

He pulled out of me. I writhed in pain. He threw a manila envelope at me.

"Open it," he demanded.

"What is it?"

"Open the fucking envelope!" he shouted.

When I looked inside, there were photos of Virginia leaving my apartment. Some were pictures that looked like they were taken directly outside my window while we were fucking. There had to be at least forty pictures.

"I noticed all of a sudden she was making random purchases for camera and studio equipment. That made me suspicious that she was seeing another guy. So, I had her followed. I never thought she would stoop this low to risk fucking up both of our lives for a piece of shit like you."

I wobbled as I stood up and slowly stepped directly in his face. "Who the fuck are you calling a piece of shit?"

He roughly jabbed his index finger in the middle of my forehead and pushed me back. The force was so hard that I thought my neck was going to snap. I fell onto the sofa.

"Shut up and listen closely," he said.

I was furious. I wasn't going to let this dickhead talk down to me. "I'm sorry your pride is hurt, but your wife likes girls. You can have all the money in the world and try to fuck her until she's raw, but what you have between your legs will never compare to me. *I* have the power."

"Power? What power do you think you have? The only person with power in this situation is *me*. After I finish here with you, I'm going to show these pictures to Virginia. I'm not going to lie and say I'm not embarrassed about this whole situation, but this gives me more leverage with her. Her family would be ruined if word got out that their little girl was a closet lesbo. They would do anything to keep me quiet. As of now, you're done seeing my wife."

"What makes you think you can stop me from seeing her?"

"I figured you would ask that. You're so arrogant that you think that you can't be touched in this whole situation, but you're highly mistaken. By the way, how is your friend Jaime doing?"

My eyes widened.

"Ah, you didn't think I knew about her, huh? I know all about the little job Virginia got her. As easy as it was to get her the job, it would be just as easy for me to take it away. I know your friend isn't qualified for that position. I know your friend has a criminal record. I can have them fire her on the grounds that she lied on her résumé alone. Now, are we going to continue to play this game, Isis?"

While I wanted to fire back at the asshole, I couldn't risk doing something that would fuck up Jaime's life.

"Fuck you!"

"Oh, I plan on fucking you right after I make my point. All of that camera and studio equipment was bought with *my* credit card, and I never approved those purchases. I'm very connected. All I have to do is say you stole the shit, and your ass will be locked up . . . *again*."

"Again?" I asked.

"Oh, you don't think I did my research on you, Isis? Or should I call you Samantha Miller? Which do you prefer?"

I was speechless.

"Whatever power you thought you had, I hope you realize now that you don't have shit. You're nothing. You're *less* than nothing. You're merely a toy that Virginia and I play with to get our rocks off."

He grabbed me and tried hard to turn me around, but I fought with him.

"If you don't stop, I swear to God I'll get your ass locked up, and your friend fired today. Now, shut up, bend over, and take this dick like the good little slut that you are."

I trembled. Feelings of rage, fear, hurt, and helplessness ran through me. I wanted to fight him. I wanted not to give in, but he was right. His words rattled me to my core and brought me back to the reality that while I thought *I* had power, I was still that poor little girl that was powerless.

My eyes glistened with tears as I stopped struggling and bent over.

"*This* is power," he said, then spit on the condom.

He rammed himself back inside me. His dick seemed to get harder at the sight of seeing me crying and obeying his wishes. He grabbed my waist; his balls smacked against my ass as he gave me forceful, repeated thrusts with all his might into my anus. I was dry. It was painful, and I bled. I think the sight of that turned him on more because the speed of his thrusts kept increasing. I gritted my teeth and bore the pain, closing my eyes and imagining I was somewhere else to escape the situation until the deed was done. I thought back to the day when Sasha and I were at the Pride parade and how happy we both were. I thought about how happy she made me and all the good times we've had until he finally came.

He slapped my ass and collapsed on top of me panting. Once he caught his breath, he shoved me away from him. He stood up and walked over to where his pants and brief-case were. He rummaged in his pants pocket and pulled out his billfold that had a wad of money in it.

"Here's your little two grand . . . with interest," he said.

He threw the money in my face and walked back to the briefcase.

"Stay the fuck away from my wife. We're both done playing with you."

He got dressed and left me balled up on the sofa in the fetal position. I held myself, rocked, and cried.

***

"You all right in there, Isis?" the bouncer asked.

The bouncers changed so often that I never attempted to learn their names. He peeked his head inside and saw I was naked on the couch. Small drops of blood were on the floor and sofa. He turned his head, trying not to stare at my nakedness. I held in my cries and pulled myself together.

"I'm all right. I just need a minute," I told him.

"You sure? You don't sound all right. If something's up, let me know, and I'll handle it."

"Everything's fine. Sometimes customers get a little too excited when they have me all to themselves." I attempted to joke about the matter.

He didn't laugh, and neither did I.

"I'm here if you need me."

I waved him off. My legs felt like Jell-O as I tried to steady myself and gain my composure. Once I finally mustered the strength to stand, I propped myself up against the sofa, got dressed, and headed for the bar. I wanted to drink until my physical and mental pain diminished. I looked around the tables and saw Mr. Smith getting a lap dance from Sapphire. He and Tyrone were grinning and laughing. Mr. Smith looked up at me, nodded, and winked. I gave him the finger and stomped over to the bar. In a perfect world, I wanted so badly to tell the cops that he raped me. I would love to see him get charged with the crime, sent to prison, and know that the inmates in there would be giving him the same treatment he gave me tonight . . . but we didn't live in a perfect world. There was no one I could go to for help. Who was I going to tell, the cops? The police never took the word of a stripper seriously when it came to rape allegations.

Besides that, I'm sure the fact that he paid me would come out and that would destroy any case I made about being raped. For the second time tonight, I would just have to take it up the ass, figuratively speaking this time, and deal with it.

I made my way through the crowd of men trying to grab my ass and made a beeline toward the bar.

"Sasha, I need a drink . . . something strong."

"Anything specific?"

"Only dark liquors."

"Damn. Rough night?"

I nodded.

"You okay?"

"No, but I will be after eight or nine drinks."

"Do you want to talk about it?"

"Nope."

Sasha handed me a Long Island Iced Tea. The strong aroma of alcohol flooded my nostrils. I took a sip of the drink. Sasha made them strong as shit. I enjoyed the warm, burning feeling that traveled throughout my body. I would only need two or three of them bad boys to be inebriated to the point of forgetting what had occurred here tonight. I picked up my drink and downed it in two gulps. Sasha handed me another.

"What happened?" she asked.

I took a big gulp of my second drink. "Nothing."

"Nope. I want to know what's up. Can I sleep over at your house tonight?"

I shrugged.

Sasha scanned the club, searching to see what had me so upset. "I know something's wrong. You were there for me when I was going through my drama. Let me be there for you."

"I appreciate it, but I would rather gouge my eyes out than look like a pathetic pussy in front of you."

"I'm just going to keep bugging you until you tell me."

"Ugh, if I agree to let you sleep over, will you drop it, please?"

"For now, but I still want to know."

"Maybe one day."

I avoided talking about what happened and continued getting shit-faced at the bar. Several drinks later, I was leaned up outside with my back against the club drunk as hell, and the club was closing for the night.

"I hate when this bitch gets sloppy. I didn't hire her to sit at the bar all night. When she gets like this, I lose money because she's too fucked up to put in work in the VIP rooms. The less she does, the less of a cut I get, and that's bad for business," Jerrod complained.

"Can you have a little compassion? She's had a rough night," Sasha said, defending me.

"Rough night—whatever. Get this drunken bitch out of here before she starts stripping out here for free. And you'd better not have been giving her any of my top-shelf shit. If I find out you did, all that shit is coming out of *your* check," Jerrod said.

"I didn't, Jerrod. Relax. Have a good night. I'll take care of her."

"I ain't worried about her." Jerrod headed toward his car.

Sasha turned and faced me. "You know you're not driving yourself home, right?"

I was staggering all over the place. I could barely stand up.

"I'm . . . fine. I can totally drive," I said, my speech slurred.

"No, you're not. I'll drive you home. Where are your keys?"

I attempted to rummage through my purse, but in my drunken state, I couldn't find shit.

"Where's your car?" I asked.

"I had to give it up. I couldn't afford it anymore."

"Damn, I'm sorry, babe. You should've asked me if you needed some loot."

Sasha grabbed my purse from my hands right before I threw up all over the parking lot. While I leaned against her shoulder, she found my keys and helped me to my car. Sasha placed me in the backseat. While she was driving, I felt even sicker to my stomach.

"Roll the window down!" I yelled.

Sasha lowered the window just in time. I threw up again as soon as she opened it. Sasha fumbled through my glove compartment, then tossed me some napkins to wipe my mouth. I patted my sweaty forehead.

"Ugh! Keep the window down. The fresh air might stop me from throwing up again."

When we got to my place, Sasha helped me to my door. I felt the vomit bubbling up in the pit of my stomach. I rushed, bounced off walls, staggered, and tripped my way into the bathroom. I went straight for the toilet, dropped to my knees, gripping the toilet with both hands to steady myself and aim before I puked. I couldn't control the vomit that spewed from my mouth as it made its way up my throat. My head spun around in circles. Sasha ran after me. She consoled me by rubbing my back and helped me up from the floor. She wiped my face, stripped me down to my bra and panties, and put me in my bed. I made a mental note to thank her in the morning because right then, I was useless.

***

I know I was dreaming, but I couldn't wake myself from the nightmare. I wanted these fucking images out of my head.

"Grab me that lube, yo," the dark-skinned man with cornrows told his Hispanic friend.

"Please don't do this," I begged them, but they didn't give a shit about my pleas.

The Hispanic guy tossed him a bottle of KY as he tried to force his dick in my mouth.

No matter how routine this became, I always cried. I hated being touched by those gross men. Joan did her usual junkie nod. The dark-skinned guy spread my vaginal lips. I screamed just as he was about to penetrate me.

***

"Sam . . . Sam . . . Sam . . ." Sasha called me, jolting me from out of my nightmare.

I shrieked in fear.

"Sam, calm down. It's me, Sasha."

Tears poured from my eyes. I shook in a cold sweat. The dream left me mortified. I blinked my eyes rapidly to get them to focus. I squinted, looking through cloudy eyes at the sight of Sasha holding me. She tried her best to console me.

"Everything is okay. It's over now. I'm here with you."

I wept in her arms. I felt like a punk for looking weak in front of her. My embarrassment made me cry harder. Sasha was gentle with me. She stroked my face and held me tightly like she would never let me go.

"Do you want to talk about it? You scared me a little bit. I was worried about you."

I had never been the type to look soft in front of a woman who I was trying to fuck, but after nightmares, I always felt emotional. I told her everything from being molested as a child, raped in jail, fucking people at the gentlemen's club, to the trauma I experienced earlier. I thought she would've looked at me weirdly once she found out all of those horrors about my past and the other shit, but she cried. She cried for me. She shared my angst.

"I'm sorry you had to go through all of that alone. I wish I knew you back when all that stuff started so I could've helped you," she said, hugging me.

"Thank you."

"I wasn't there back then, but I'm here for you now. Will you let me help you?"

"What do you mean?"

"On campus, they always have flyers for RAINN, which stands for Rape, Abuse, Incest National Network. I think you should go to a rape survivor meeting."

"Are you fucking crazy? I'm not going to sit with a bunch of fucking strangers and tell my business."

"I'll go with you. You won't be alone. Do you want to continue to have these dreams, or do you want to try to work this shit out?"

I wanted to say no. I didn't want to air my dirty laundry to a group of strangers. Only a very choice few knew about it, and I intended on taking my shitty, rape-involved childhood to the grave with me. I had every intention of telling her a hard "hell no," but when Sasha looked at me, I knew everything was from the heart. Hearing the sincerity in her words and knowing she genuinely wanted to help me gave me the courage to at least check out a few meetings.

Eight

Hi, My Name Is Samantha

Sasha did some research the next day after I confided in her. The following week, we went to the next
scheduled rape survivors' meeting. The meetings were
held in Manhattan on 122nd Street. The first couple of
meetings, I sat there with Sasha and listened to everyone
talk. I didn't have the courage to say anything. Listening
to their stories always got me worked up emotionally.
Their stories made me think of my own experiences. I
was angry at my mother, angry at the men who raped me.
Angry that I was too weak and powerless to stop it from
happening. Lastly, I was sad that I had to go through that
bullshit.

There were people of all ages, races, and social back-
grounds at the meeting. It surprised me when a couple of
straight men explained their painful experiences of being
raped. I found comfort in hearing and knowing that other
people went through similar emotions and experiences
as I. The information at the meetings made me think and
reflect on my past a lot. I was dealing with my own issues
better, and my nightmares weren't as severe as they had
been in the past.

At the sixth meeting, the counselor, Dr. John Andrews,
asked me if I would like to share with the group.

"Samantha, you've been a part of this group for a while now, coming to meetings and hearing other members sharing their stories. Would you care to share your story with the rest of the group? Talking about it helps us all to heal," he said, pushing his glasses up over the bridge of his nose.

"Not a fucking chance," I said.

"Sam!" Sasha protested.

I turned to her. "I'll listen to everyone else's story, but there is no way in hell I'm going to air my business out to a bunch of strangers. Fuck, no."

Some of the people in the group looked offended by what I said, but I didn't give a shit. A very selective few knew about my past, and that was just fine with me.

"Samantha, it's therapeutic to everyone if we all share with the group. It helps us all to see that we're not alone and helps us develop a stronger support system for one another."

"Nope. It's not happening." I stood up. "This shit isn't for me," I said.

I wanted to get up and run the fuck out, but Sasha held my hand, rubbed it, looked me in the eyes, and gently guided me back down to my seat. "Sam, don't run away. Talk to them. Everything is going to be okay. I'm right here with you," she said.

I sighed.

"Hi, everyone. My name is Samantha Miller, and I . . . I . . . I can't do this."

I attempted to get up to leave again, but Sasha held on to me and pulled me back down to my seat again.

"It's okay. Just start off slow. They've all been through the same things you've been through or worse," Sasha whispered to me.

"Again, welcome, Samantha. We've all enjoyed having you at the couple of meetings you've been to. We want you to know that we're all here for you, and this is a safe place. We all share similar pain," Dr. Andrews said.

"With all due respect, you all might have been raped too, but trust me when I tell you, none of you have had pain like I have had."

"Help us understand," Dr. Andrews said.

I didn't know how comfortable I could be divulging my deepest and darkest secrets to the group.

Normally, I wouldn't be caught dead talking to a doctor, male or female, about being raped, but after numerous occasions of hearing him share his personal stories of being raped and abused by his uncle, I felt more comfortable. He was a dark-skinned brother in his early 50s—a widower with three college-age daughters. His comments were always deep and meaningful. Whenever he spoke, his words made me think.

I started off slow, telling them about some of the horrors I went through being raped throughout my childhood, not really feeling the need to go all into details with the group.

"What do y'all want to hear? I've been on my own since I was 14. My mother was a junkie prostitute named Joan, who was addicted to heroin and eventually died from AIDS because of sharing needles. My childhood was not even close to being normal. Most kids had a decent place to stay and kids to play with. My mother and I were thrown out of numerous roach- and rat-infested apartments and bounced from homeless shelter to homeless shelter. Most mothers taught their daughters how to cook. My mother taught me how to escape to a different part of my mind when a pedophile was fucking me.

When her habit got too big, she pimped me out to clients because they offered to pay her double her usual amount to fuck her kid."

Some of the women covered their mouths. Some of the men shook their heads as I continued.

"The first time I was deflowered on a piss-stained mattress in an abandoned, rat-infested U-Haul truck. The man's gold-toothed smile still haunts me in my dreams to this day. He didn't care that I was a 10-year-old kid. He savagely ripped off my panties and had his way with me."

Tears formed in my eyes, but I wiped them away with the back of my hand before they fell.

I didn't think I would ever reveal so much of myself to the group and tell them things with such detail. I figured I would keep shit short and brief and let everyone else tell all their business, but the words kept flowing out of my mouth.

"When it was over, I was bleeding. I was sore. I was traumatized. I curled up in a ball and wanted to die. I wished that it was all a bad dream, but this was my reality. My faith in humanity and a part of me died that day. My childhood ended in that U-Haul truck. I wanted my mom to hold me, to comfort me. I wanted her to tell me that it would never happen again and that she loved me, but that would never be the case. She sat there nodding out while he pulled up his pants and left us there. Since then, I've always bathed in water that was borderline scalding hot because no matter how much I washed, I still felt dirty and violated. After the first time, it became easier for my mother to sell me to the highest bidder for sexual favors. There were so many times when I gritted my teeth, closed my eyes, and prayed that they would just come quick."

I was determined not to lose my shit completely in front of my therapy group. I took a deep breath and wiped my face.

"My whole life, all people have wanted to do was fuck me. I felt like I was nothing, and the only thing I was good for was lying on my back for sex. My mother died when I was 14. When I sought out my father, praying that he would take me in, so I wasn't homeless, he beat my ass in the street and threatened to 'break me in' and pimp me out if I didn't get out of his face. I had no other skills, so I did the only thing I was good at . . . prostitution. I got arrested by the cops numerous times and was sentenced to do a bid at the Albion Correctional Facility upstate. The correction officers used to sneak into my cell late at night and rape me. I had inmates in prison that tried to hold me down and rape me in the shower. Every time I was raped, I felt like a part of my soul rotted away. Now, I feel like I don't have much of a soul left."

The tears were flowing from my eyes. Fuck it. I was tired of trying to fight back the tears from falling down my face.

"It's . . ." I stopped myself midsentence and wiped the tears from my face. "It's hard to talk about. Look at me, crying like a big pussy in front of a bunch of strangers."

I was waiting for them to start judging me and to look at me like I was a piece of shit, but their expressions didn't look judgmental. They looked more sympathetic.

Many of the members cried when they heard my story. I didn't tell everything, but I told them the basics. Sasha nodded with tears in her eyes and winked at me. I exhaled and relaxed my shoulders. I felt like a weight had been lifted off of them. This was a big step for me. It was hard opening up to people, especially a group of strangers, and I wouldn't have ever done that in the past.

As time went on, I confided more and more in the group. I made it a priority to attend the meetings, and even though Sasha didn't have to, she always showed her support by going to the meetings with me. Having her there gave me the strength to deal with the shit I kept hidden deep down in my soul.

I told Silka and Jaime everything about the group, Dr. Andrews, and Sasha's support. They noticed my more upbeat demeanor, agreed that going to the meetings was a good thing, and that Sasha was one of the most positive people in my life at the time.

"She really cares about you, Sam. Maybe you should look at her as more than a fuck," Jaime said.

"I'm with Jaime on this one. She rearranges her school and work schedules to go to the meetings with you. That says a lot," Silka added.

"I know, that does speak volumes. I care about her, so when I do bed her, it will be more than a fuck for me."

"So, despite everything, you still see her as a conquest?" Jaime asked.

"Nah. I stopped seeing her as a conquest when she went to the Gay Pride Parade with me. Sasha going to the meetings with me only reinforces it in my mind more that I want a genuine relationship with her. She makes me feel like I could have a monogamous relationship and be happy and faithful. I haven't felt this way before about anyone. I thought I loved Cheryl, but this is different. It feels good and real."

"Well, congratulations, Sam. You're finally getting a taste of what it feels like to be in love," Silka said.

I still danced at the club, but since I had been going to the meetings and picking up more business with my photography, I only worked the minimum amount of time necessary to stay employed there.

My nightmares weren't entirely gone, but they weren't as frequent as they usually were. Dr. Andrews counseled me both privately and through group sessions. When we first started, I didn't trust him when he said he wanted to counsel me both in the groups and privately. In the group sessions, he always seemed like a decent guy, but I met many motherfuckers who looked nice on the outside and turned out to be perverted assholes. I wasn't sure of his motives, and I figured he wasn't any different from all the other men I met all my life. I remember the first time I went to his office.

"Good evening, Samantha. I'm glad you could make it," Dr. Andrews greeted, seeming excited to see me.

I walked into his office, and he motioned for me to sit down. His quaint office was decorated with nice wooden furniture and many pictures of him with gay activists and celebrities. Beautiful African sculptures covered his desk and bookshelves.

He was sitting behind his desk, preparing his notes for the next group discussion. I sighed and mentally prepared myself for another douche bag who just wanted to get a piece of ass. I sat slumped down in the chair across from him. I purposely wore a tight skirt.

"Yeah yeah yeah. So, what is this about? If you want to fuck me, it's going to cost you. I'm not cheap."

Dr. Andrews frowned. Lines formed on his forehead. The scowl on his face showed I pissed him off.

"I didn't call you here for anything like that."

"Look, when it comes down to it, all you men want to do is fuck me. So, let's save ourselves the song and dance."

I uncrossed my legs to show him that I wasn't wearing any panties. I smiled at him.

"Do you like what you see?"

"Stop it!" Dr. Andrews looked like he wanted to go off on me. Instead, he took a deep breath, calmed his nerves, and continued. "In order for me to help you heal, you have to know that not every man you meet is out to hurt you. I know it's difficult for you to believe that when you've experienced so much pain, but I promise you—even if I'm the only exception—I will never betray your trust. I don't want anything from you. The only thing I want is for you to get better."

Calling his bluff, I stood up and walked up to his chair. I pulled my shirt off, showing him my bare breasts.

"Come on, Doctor. I know you want to fuck me. It's okay. I've seen the way you look at me. Admitting it to yourself will save both of us a lot of time."

I sat on his lap and kissed the side of his face. He reacted by pushing me to the floor.

"Samantha, stop! I don't want to touch you in that manner, and I never will. I only want to help you."

Despite what he said, I noticed he had an erection.

"Your mouth is saying no, but your body is saying the opposite."

"Samantha, stop it now!"

"What's wrong? Don't you like what you see? If you're into guys and like pegging, I can get my strap-on and fuck you properly. If you prefer to be a giver and not a taker, I can bend over and let you fuck me in my ass. You can take out all of that pent-up aggravation from when your uncle raped you out on me."

His nostrils flared. If I couldn't get him to admit he wanted to fuck me, I would piss him off enough so that his true colors would show.

Dr. Andrews shook his head. "Samantha, you are a confused and damaged young woman. I can tell you're good at manipulating people, but deep down, the person who really gets hurt by your actions is you. You are wounded. Instead of accepting my willingness to help and not betray your trust, you immediately tried to discredit me."

His words bothered me. He continued.

"When you realized you couldn't seduce me, you tried to use my anger as a means of getting me to go back on what I just promised. Deep down, you want to be helped, but you're so broken you don't know how to accept it. How does that make you feel, Samantha? How does it feel to know I can see through your manipulation, and you can't use sex as a means of controlling me?"

I got up off the floor and glared at him as he continued to talk. I thought about all of the men I had met in my life. I thought of how they had all hurt me, and then I looked at him. What made him special? What made him any different? I was tired of all the bullshit men had told me.

"In your nightmares, do you feel like you're in control, or do you feel powerless?" he asked.

"Shut up! Shut up! Shut up!"

I balled up my fists and charged at him. Dr. Andrews stood up and dodged my first punch. My eyes welled up with tears because I knew everything he was saying was true. I pounded on his chest. Each blow weakened in force until I broke down crying in his arms.

"Samantha, let me help you. Let's continue our session and get to the root of your pain so I can help you heal. It won't be an easy or a quick fix, but no matter how long it takes, I'll be here for you."

I nodded, and we continued with our session.

After that day, we talked often. What I enjoyed most about our conversations was that he was straight up with me. I admired his ability to read and understand me. It was those qualities that made me respect him and trust him more. As time went on, he helped me to understand myself better.

Nine

Fierce

I sat in Dr. Andrews's office. He told me that he wanted to counsel me privately about something he felt hindered my growth. He sat at his desk with his hands together and stared intently at me through his thick, round-framed glasses.

"Samantha, do you believe being raped has affected your relationship with women?"

"Hell nah, I love women."

"You love to pleasure women. You love the feeling of power it gives you, but you don't love those women."

"I guess not, but what does that have to do with being raped by men, Dr. Andrews?"

"You know, you can call me John, right? You don't have to be so formal."

"Nah, I don't like your name. 'John' sounds like the men that used to fuck me. Calling you 'Dr. Andrews' makes me feel safe. Anyway, what do you mean that being raped by men has affected my relationship with women?"

"You show a few signs that being raped has affected you. You have a mild case of PTSD, post-traumatic stress disorder. Your sleep disturbances are a big telltale sign. Plus, you've been suicidal in the past."

"Okay, but what does that have to do with it?"

"Another effect rape can have on a person is substance abuse."

"I don't use drugs! I've told you that!" I was insulted by his insinuation.

"No, you substitute drugs with a different kind of addiction—women. Have you ever been in a committed relationship? Not like a friendship or merely a sexual partner, but a monogamous relationship?"

"No."

"Why do you think that is?"

"I don't know. I've never really been the relationship type. I haven't had much interest in being tied down to one person like that. I get bored with women easily."

Dr. Andrews leaned back in his chair, his gaze unyielding and questioning.

"You might not believe it, but your past has affected how you treat women now. You have a huge disdain for men because of what some have done to you and the things you've seen them do to other women, but in reality, you do some of the same things that you hate. You say you learned a lot from Cheryl, but your feelings for her are still bittersweet. Do you realize you are treating women the same way Cheryl treated you?"

He continued to stare at me, giving his words a chance to sink in. I fidgeted in his cushioned wooden office chair. He stated a lot of things I already knew but didn't want to admit to myself.

"How do you think some of those women feel when you have sex with them and leave them? Do you think every woman you leave questioning their sexuality will end up having a positive experience?"

"I'm not trying to hurt anyone. I only look for women who I feel are already on the cusp."

"Do you feel Sasha is on the cusp?"

I looked down at the multicolored area rug. Sometimes talking with him made me feel like a scolded child, and I hated that.

God, I wanted a fucking cigarette.

"Yes," I responded timidly.

"I think she is, also, but she's scared. We all evolve into the people we're supposed to be, but it's a long, drama-filled road to get to that point. She adores you. She looks up to you, but I think she fears what the future would hold with you. I know you care about her, and I know she cares about you. I think the key to helping you heal would be to have a committed relationship with someone you truly love, and I believe Sasha is that person for you. For that to happen, you have to open your heart and let people in. Don't let your addiction to women push Sasha away. She has helped you tremendously with your progress so far. Don't let your problems with commitment hinder that."

"What about my friends? I'm committed to them."

"That's true, but you don't want to sleep with them."

He had a point.

"I want you to think long and hard. From what you've told me privately of how you've been with women in the past, do you want to risk losing Sasha—someone you care about and who legitimately cares about you—or will you make her another victim?"

His words hit me. Even after our group meeting, all I could think about was what he asked me.

Sasha took the train to the group meeting. I promised to drive her back to the Bronx once it was over.

"What's on your mind that has you so deep in thought? You've barely said anything the entire ride," Sasha asked.

"Dr. Andrews mentioned something to me during our private session that's making me question things, that's all."

"He's done that to me too on a couple of occasions," Sasha laughed. "What did he say? What are you questioning?"

In reality, I questioned a lot of things. I questioned if I even wanted to fuck Sasha and turn her out anymore. I questioned if she even had romantic feelings for me. I questioned if I loved her, but most importantly, I questioned if what I felt was real. I didn't want to waste my time if it wasn't.

"I don't want to get into it right now. I'll tell you later."

Sasha opened her mouth like she wanted to delve deeper into the topic but stopped herself. "Okay," she said.

"Do you want to get something to eat?" I asked.

"Yeah. I haven't eaten anything all day."

"Why?"

"I'm broke."

"Why don't you ask your parents for money? You know they'd give it to you. Shit, they're not struggling. They have money."

"My parents baby me enough as it is. If I let them support me financially, they would never look at me as being an adult. I would still be a child in their eyes. I want to live my life and make my own decisions. If I allow them to support me, they will still think they can control every aspect of my life."

"I get it. Well, I'll treat your broke ass to Applebee's," I teased.

Sasha rolled her eyes. "Oh, thanks. That didn't make me feel like a bum at all."

We laughed. Sasha placed her hand on mine. All of the signs were there. I knew there was an attraction, but I wasn't sure if I could or even wanted to be in a committed relationship.

Sasha and I walked into Applebee's holding hands. The waiter seated us at our table. He was clearly "family." He was a thin, gangly black guy with wide eyes and a sensual walk that rivaled mine.

"Here's your table, girls, and let me tell y'all, you ladies look fierce together," he commented.

I smiled, but Sasha quickly got defensive.

"No, no . . . We're not together. We're just friends," she said.

I looked at her, and my eyes tightened. The waiter noticed my expression.

"Oh, I'm sorry about that. Well, you ladies both look beautiful today."

"Thank you," Sasha replied.

Our waiter walked away. I felt angry and embarrassed. Sasha noticed I was visibly upset.

"What's the matter?"

I looked at her like she was stupid. There was so much I wanted to say, but I buried my head in my menu.

"If you don't get why I'm upset, then nothing is the matter."

"Did I do something wrong?" she asked innocently.

I knew she didn't make that comment maliciously, but my feelings and everything Dr. Andrews brought up earlier was fucking with me.

"I'm just PMSing," I said, calming myself. "It's nothing. I'm just overly sensitive today."

Sasha looked concerned but didn't press.

It wasn't long until our food came, and we were back to acting like our usual selves. While I gave her the illusion that nothing was wrong with me, I needed to fuck a girl. I spent so much time trying to entice Sasha that I was neglecting my own needs. As soon as I took her home, I planned to find some random girl and get my rocks off.

Dr. Andrews was right. I enjoyed the power I got from fucking women. That wasn't going to change . . . and neither was I.

"Oooh . . . yes . . . shit! Don't fucking stop! Just like that. Oooh!" Gelissa moaned.

The muscles in my forearm pulsed as I relentlessly thrust three fingers into her sopping pussy. With my free hand, I pressed on her clit, firmly circling over it with the tips of my fingers.

"Mmm, oh God! Don't stop! Please, don't stop," Gelissa begged.

I felt her walls contract. Her back arched, and a wave of come gushed out of her convulsing vagina. She climaxed with such intensity that her muscles flexed, and her knees locked. Gelissa whimpered and moaned in ecstasy, relishing in the remnants of her orgasm. I wasn't done with her yet.

While she squirmed and twitched on the bed, I got up and put on my strap. I parted her legs and thrust my pelvis forward. Her eyes bulged from the length and girth of my dildo. My vagina pulsated in the harness from the combination of the friction from my thrusts and her moans. Her legs bent at the knees as I pushed them farther back, and her thighs clenched around my hips. I massaged her breasts and leaned forward while thrusting so I could place each breast in my mouth. She squeezed them together, allowing me to suckle both nipples simultaneously. My penetration was unrelenting. Her juices dripped down her legs. She squealed with delight as another orgasm rolled through her.

By the end of our fuck session, she was passed out on the motel bed. I smiled and reveled in the fact that *I did that!* I left her a simple note, which read: Thanks for the good time. Checkout is at 11:00 a.m.

I placed the note on the nightstand and left her sleeping in the room while I headed home. I wasn't totally satisfied, but my hunger was suppressed for the time being.

Earlier that evening, I dropped Sasha off at her place. We made plans to hang out in the village on Friday night with Silka and Jaime. Once she was safely in her building, I went home to change and grab a few things for my plans that evening, and then I was off to find my next victim.

I drove to Sin City, a rival strip club off Park Avenue in the Bronx. It was more upscale than the club I worked in, but it wasn't fully nude. If I worked there, I could definitely make a shit ton of money, but the competition would be tough. I didn't search for prey at my own club because after I slept with whatever girl I found, I didn't plan on ever talking to her again. Meeting someone where I worked meant they would always know where to find me. Another reason for picking a strip club to find a random woman was that no matter the day of the week, there would always be a few women on the fence.

It was time to start hunting. Step one: Find a group of girls. Lots of women find female strip clubs more exciting and fun than male ones so that part would be easy. Step two: Search for the girl with the loudest mouth. Like the show *Sex and the City,* every group of females had their version of Samantha. There was always one that was adventurous and borderline slutty. That girl in the group would be the one who frequently did spontaneous, crazy things to impress her friends. Step three: This is the hardest. I would have to identify who that girl was in the group and play with her ego. Then I would have to convince her that it would be more of a dare/challenge than me actually wanting to fuck her brains out.

I sat down at a candlelit table near the stage and searched for candidates. The club set up was more appealing than the one I worked at. There was a massive bar in the corner of the room that looked stocked with every liquor imaginable. The bar where I worked paled in comparison. The club had numerous elevated small stages decorated with circular brass railings, soft red and pink spotlights, and different girls dancing simultaneously on each stage. Around the stages were round, medium-sized tables with burgundy tablecloths and small candles.

There were three groups of women laughing, shouting, and throwing money on the stages. Two of the three groups looked like they were family, but the last group caught my eye. There she was—my next conquest. She was a beautiful Hispanic woman with an olive-colored complexion and long, silky black hair. The cosmopolitan in her hand must have amplified her loud and bossy personality. I moved closer to the group of women to observe her better.

"Didn't I tell you this place was the shit? Take notes, ladies, so you know how to move to keep your man's dick up. I should ask for an application so I can show these young girls how to really dance," she said jokingly.

She had a confidence about her that bordered on arrogance. I liked that. I listened to more of her conversation with her friends.

"So, I told him, 'You need to trim that shit.' He was like, 'Why?' I looked that fool dead in his eyes and said, 'Because I can't see the tree through the forest, fool. *That's* why!'" She was met with thunderous laughter.

"Then this dude tells me he doesn't go down. I swear I'm getting tired of these small-dick, weak men. I'm about to switch over and start fucking with girls," she continued jokingly.

That was my cue.

"Talk is cheap," I shouted to her.

"Ooooh!" her friends said in unison.

Shocked that someone would dare talk to her that way, her friends turned around. They looked me up and down, covered their mouths, and whispered to each other. She looked at her friends and then glared at me. She was clearly embarrassed, which is what I wanted. It was all part of the game.

"Do I know you? You damn sure don't know me, so who are you to comment on anything *I* say?" she responded.

"My name's Sam. I'm tired of women like you, fronting that you would fuck with a woman. Don't talk about it if you won't live it."

She smiled at me. I challenged her, and that seemed to turn her on.

"I'm Gelissa." She reached to shake my hand. "What makes you think I'm fronting about that?"

Holding her hand, I placed my other hand on top of hers and looked her in her soft brown eyes.

"If you were about that life, you would've tried it by now. You're only saying you would to look bold to your friends. Let me buy you a few drinks. After that, maybe you'll have more courage and do more than just put singles in women's thongs."

Our eye contact was strong. While she looked at me as a challenge, I only looked at her as lunch. She was playing right into my trap. I knew she wouldn't back out of fucking me because she didn't want to be showed up in front of her friends.

"Look, Sam, we're trying to have a nice girls' night together. No offense, but we don't know you. You might feel a certain way about women sleeping with other women, but take your gripes somewhere else," one of Gelissa's friends said, trying to stick up for her.

Gelissa waved her comment away. "It's cool, Maureen. Stay, Sam. You've got my attention *and* my interest. I'm sure by the end of the night I'll have you backing down."

Gelissa didn't know what she got herself into. Maureen was a cutie. She had long, well-kept dreads and wore a red, form-fitting dress that suited her petite frame. I bought Gelissa and her friends drinks. Most of the drinks went to Gelissa's friends. I made sure she didn't have too much. I wanted her to be sober for the experience, not make excuses and blame it on the alcohol.

As we watched stripper after stripper do their routine, I constantly whispered into Gelissa's ear, playing on her vanity and curiosity. Everyone drank and had a good time except for Maureen, who watched my every move like a hawk.

It didn't take long to convince Gelissa to get a room with me. By then, everyone but Maureen was drunk off their ass.

"You ready to go, or are you chickening out?" I asked Gelissa.

She looked hesitant but smiled at my taunt.

"Yep."

I didn't waste any time. Not even allowing her enough time to say goodbye to her friends, I quickly pushed her toward the exit. Out of nowhere, Maureen grabbed her arm.

"Where the fuck are you going? Can't you see she's fucking with your head?" Maureen asked.

I didn't need her shit when I was so close to getting Gelissa out of there.

"Great, here it comes. You're going to back out. I fucking knew it. Go on . . . Leave with your friend while you have a chance," I said condescendingly.

Gelissa pulled away from Maureen. "I got this. I'm a big girl. I don't need you to look out for me." Gelissa pointed toward their friends. "Take care of their drunken asses. You're sober so you can be their ride. I'm going to cross this shit off my bucket list."

"And who is going to be your ride home?"

Gelissa looked at me. I smiled to myself because she was highly mistaken if she thought she was getting a ride home from me. After our deed was done, I'd be out the door.

"You don't have anything to prove, G. She's just looking to fuck. She's playing you," Maureen said.

"Nobody plays me. I do what I want, when I want," Gelissa replied confidently.

Maureen threw her hands up and shook her head. "You know what? You can act tough now. Everyone's drunk and won't say anything, but when you get hurt like you always do, don't come crying to me."

"Don't worry; I won't. Bye!"

Maureen looked at me and asked, "Happy?"

"I will be in a few minutes after I turn out your friend," I smirked.

Maureen turned her nose up at me and slowly walked away backward before turning around and sitting down with her friends.

I looked at Gelissa. "You ready?"

"Let's do this," she said.

I was bored to death with Gelissa bragging about herself the entire ride to the Pelham Garden Motel off East Gun Hill Road. There was no way I would take her to my place because I didn't know if Sasha would somehow make a spontaneous visit and hear me fucking the shit out of this girl. While still uncertain what would come out of my relationship with Sasha, I couldn't risk losing all of the time and effort I put into courting her.

The motel wasn't the fanciest, but it would do the job. The room had a huge heart-shaped mirror mounted on the ceiling over the bed. Gelissa swiftly headed to the windows and closed the thick, white curtains. The room was dark; the only light present was the dull red lights encircling the bed's headboard.

I pulled back the thin burgundy comforter and pulled her to me. Gelissa's breathing quickened. She could lie and say she wasn't nervous, but I knew she was terrified, and that made me feel in charge. I leaned toward her and gave her a long kiss. I felt nothing, but I didn't expect to. I grabbed the back of her neck and kissed her again. My hands roamed her body while I groped and removed every article of clothing she had on—piece by piece. Her hands trembled when she undressed me. We stood next to the bed holding each other and kissing until she shoved me onto the bed and pushed my thighs open. For the moment, I let her feel like she was running the show, but soon, I would definitely show her that she was *my* bitch.

"I've never done this before," Gelissa said softly.

Under all her toughness, I saw her true self at that moment. Everything she did was a front, a defense mechanism to mask her fear of not being liked by people. She portrayed someone confident and secure, but in reality, she was timid and weak. Realizing those facts about her made me think back to my conversation with Dr. Andrews. It made me question if I was the same way. I shook those thoughts away. I didn't want to think or feel anything emotionally. I just wanted to feel powerful, to feel in control. I had pent-up anger and frustration from my feelings with Sasha. Fucking was the only way I knew how to release that shit, and turning Gelissa out would give me what I wanted.

I didn't respond to Gelissa's statement. I replied by pushing her head down and burying her face in my flower. I watched her head bob up and down as she licked and sucked my pussy. For the most part, she was decent at it, but there was no way I would reciprocate. I wasn't in the mood and from experience with bitches like Gelissa, I knew it wouldn't take much effort to wear her out.

I held her face in my treasure as I came. She emerged saturated with my juices. She wiped her face with the back of her hand. It was now time to show her how to *really* satisfy a woman.

I left Gelissa at the motel once she fell asleep. It was of no concern to me that I was her ride. My goal was accomplished; therefore, I didn't care or need her anymore. Three times that week, I went on to do this same scheme with different women at different locations. While this used to be routine and fun for me, I felt myself yearning for Sasha. I didn't enjoy doing this like I used to, but I did it anyway. I felt myself changing. I was getting soft and weak and thinking too much about Sasha's feelings and my own.

I wanted a real monogamous relationship with Sasha. My mind constantly flooded with thoughts of her, but something needed to give. Either we would talk about our future together, or I would have to cut her off as a friend. I didn't know what would happen, but I knew if I didn't get these feelings out, I would only get worse. I feared what I might do.

Ten

Joy and Pain

Sasha and I sat on the couch watching *Kissing Jessica Stein*. I didn't care too much for the movie because of how it ended, but Sasha was adamant about watching it. We had originally planned for a night of partying, but Silka couldn't make it because her baby was sick, and Jaime had to work late. We settled on ordering from Domino's and watching movies. I was in an irritable mood after our encounter with Sasha's ex, Travis, while walking into Domino's to pick up our food.

"What's up, Sasha?"

Sasha was smiling . . . until she realized who had spoken to her. The smile instantly left her face.

"Hi, Travis," she said dismissively.

His eyes traveled up and down her body. "You're looking good," he added.

"Thanks."

I let them talk but watched her body language the whole time. Sasha wouldn't look him in the face. She kept tapping her foot. She let out an annoyed sigh and blew out a heavy gust of air from her nostrils. She was clearly bothered. I walked up to them.

"You okay?" I asked.

"She's fine," Travis said.

"I wasn't talking to you, and I for damn sure didn't ask you."

Not bothering to look in his direction, I kept my attention focused on Sasha and placed my hand on the small of her back.

"I'm fine," she responded softly.

"Do you want to get food somewhere else? I don't mind. Let me know, and I'll cancel the order here."

"Nah, I'm good."

Travis picked up on our body language. He smiled, looking back and forth from Sasha and me and stared at her.

"So, what's this? We break up, and you start fucking bitches now? You couldn't find a man good enough to replace me, huh?"

Sasha was furious. "Don't flatter yourself. She's just my friend, and being free from you was the best thing that could have ever happened to me and *my wallet. Where's* your *bitch? Did she drop your ass after she realized* she'd *have to support* you?*"*

I thought with her last dis he would back off, but he played on her sensitivity of being my girlfriend.

"Wow! Word, Sasha? You're right . . . She left me, but let's forget about all that. Let's go back to our old place, and the three of us can have a good weekend. From the look of things, your face is already in this chick's box. So I'll just supply the dick. I know you don't want me back, but the least you can do is let me fuck one last time with you and *your girlfriend. What do you say?"*

"Fuck you, Travis!" Sasha screamed.

"Look here, you bitch-ass nig—" I said before being interrupted.

"Whoa! Sasha, call your lady off. I don't fight girls. Do your parents know you're eating pussy? They hated me, so I know this must drive them Bible-thumping asses crazy."

Sasha's eyes got tight. She said nothing, but I saw her anger building up. She was about to explode any second. Travis just chuckled at her.

"Oh shit! You mean they don't *know? Wow! Well, it's good to know I'm the last brother to hit that. If it means anything, at least you have good taste. Your bitch is fine!"*

I stepped up to him. I wanted to punch him in the fucking mouth, but Sasha held me back. She let me know this wasn't my war.

"Stay out of this, Sam. I can handle my own battles."

Any other day I would have put this guy in his place, but I was more upset with Sasha. Why would it have been so bad if she were with me? Why was she so close to me, but whenever anyone looked at her as being gay, she freaked out? These "freak-outs" were getting old fast. I didn't know how much more I would be able to take.

"Oh, shit . . . and her name is Sam too. So, she's the butch, and you're the bitch? That's funny," Travis laughed. He turned to me.

"You are the man in the relationship, right?"

Before I could answer, Sasha shouted out, *"She's* not *my fucking girlfriend!"* Her nostrils flared as she clenched her fists. I had never seen her look so angry.

"I get it . . . I get it. I meant boyfriend. *I know she's the top . . . My mistake,"* he laughed again.

"Oooh! I fucking hate you! You make me sick!" Sasha screamed.

All of the employees at Domino's smiled, enjoying the show. They motioned to him that his order was ready.

"Well, my food is ready. I'm about to be out, but, Sasha, you got my number. If you and your friend here want to get together sometime, hit a brother up."

He grabbed his bags and pizza box, laughed at us, and walked out. Sasha was fuming. When she looked at my face, it registered with her that I was hurt by her comments.

"Sam, I'm sorry I acted like that. He brings out the worst in me."

I paid the cashier and grabbed our food. "Don't worry about it."

We came back to my place, and like serendipity, Kissing Jessica Stein was on cable. Still annoyed with what happened, I didn't say much. Sasha was nuzzled comfortably on my chest.

"What would you consider yourself?" Sasha asked, her eyes glued to the movie.

"What do you mean?"

"Do you consider yourself a stud, a femme, or some other type I've learned about from hanging with you?"

"If I would call myself anything, I'd say I was an aggressive femme, but I'm at a point in my life where I don't use labels anymore. I know what I like, I know what I want, and I don't need a title to define who I am."

Sasha nodded. My words were meant more as a statement than an answer to her question.

"What's it like?"

In my head, I beamed with delight at the fact that she was asking questions about being with women. Maybe she was starting to come around.

"What's what like?" I asked, playing dumb.

"You know . . . being with a woman."

"Why are you asking me that?"

"I don't know. I guess I'm just curious to know what it's like."

"It's great. Being with a woman is light-years better than being with a man. No man can know a woman's body better than a woman, but being with a woman goes beyond physical needs. Because we're both women, our thoughts and emotions are somewhat similar. We understand each other better than a man would. So many women live their lives unfulfilled being with a man who doesn't fully understand how to please them in every aspect. It's easier when you're with a woman."

Sasha looked up and kissed me on the cheek. I faced her, lifted her chin, and kissed her directly on the mouth. She wrapped her arms around my neck and got lost in our kiss. Unexpectedly, Sasha gasped. She stopped kissing me, removed her arms, and pushed me off her.

I looked at her questioningly.

"I . . . I can't," Sasha said, her voice wavering.

"Stop fucking playing with my head! I'm so sick of this shit!"

"Sick of what? What am I doing?"

"Don't play dumb with me. I'm tired of playing games. You're touchy with me and always flirt with me. You ask me all these questions, get me all worked up, and then you pull this shit?"

Sasha became defensive. *"If I act that way, it's your fault. You introduced me to your lifestyle and have me questioning everything. You're manipulative. I never questioned my sexuality until I met you."*

"If you have questions about it, you're probably suppressing who you really are. I'm not doing shit but being who I am. I'm not telling you what you should do . . . nature is."

"No, I'm not a lesbian. You have me all fucking confused."

"I'm so tired of you 'fake straights' playing games—fucking around with women when it's convenient for you." I grabbed her arm. Sasha moved back and tried to pull away from me.

"Look at me!" I yelled.

"No!"

"Look at me!"

Sasha stopped struggling and stared me in the face.

"Do you want *me? Are your feelings for me deeper than friendship? I want you. I want to be with you. I'm in love with you. Look me in my eyes and tell me you don't feel the same way."*

Her face wore an expression of sadness and confusion. She looked down and shook her head.

"No . . . I don't have those feelings for you. Stop putting thoughts in my head. What you're asking me for goes against my religion and my family. I can't give you what you're asking me for," she responded, her voice cracking.

Her response made me livid. *"Fuck your religion!"* I lashed back. *"Fuck your family! If you're going to lie to yourself and me about how you feel, and you think I'm putting these thoughts in your head, get the fuck out of my house and out of my life. I don't have time for this shit. I'm tired of wasting my time with you."*

I stomped toward the door, opened it, and motioned for her to get out. Sasha slowly gathered her things.

"Hurry up! Get the fuck out!"

As soon as both her feet were in the hallway, I slammed the door. The sound echoed throughout the halls. I stormed into the bedroom and rummaged through the top dresser drawer in search of my emergency stash of cig-

arettes. I grabbed my lighter next to the pack and rested the cigarette between my lips while I attempted to light it, but my lighter wouldn't work. For some strange reason, the desire to smoke made me feel guilty. I threw the lighter and pack of cigarettes into my drawer and kicked it shut. I was annoyed at myself that even while I was furious with Sasha, I wanted to keep my promise to her. I loved her, but if she wasn't willing to return that love, I had to let her go. It took me a long time to open up my heart to someone again, and I was tired of having it played with.

I lay across my couch, staring at the ceiling. The sounds of heavy raindrops hitting my window soothed my conflicted soul. I used to be self-assured, but lately, things in my life had me questioning myself.

Suddenly, I heard a light knock at the door, but I wasn't in the mood for company. I contemplated remaining quiet and ignoring it, but then I decided to see who it was. I forced myself to get up, reluctantly hopped to my feet, and looked through the peephole to see who it was. I opened the door. Sasha stood there soaking wet with tears in her eyes. I exhaled and stepped aside to let her walk in.

"I'm sorry I said those things. I didn't mean them."

I sighed. "I didn't mean the shit I said either. I really want a fucking cigarette, and I'm an irritable bitch right now." I chuckled, but Sasha's eyes filled with more tears.

"I . . . I . . . I need to know," she cried, looking down at her feet and wringing her hands.

I knew what she was curious about, but I wanted to hear her say it out loud. "What exactly do you feel you need to know?"

"I have all of these feelings. I have all of these thoughts running through my head. I need to know if what I'm feeling is curiosity or if it's what I truly want. I don't want to do this with anyone else. If I'm going to find out the answers to my questions, I want those answers to come from being with you."

Sasha looked so confused. I had won. I accomplished my goal, but this victory was hollow. I loved Sasha, and while I could easily achieve my goal of bedding her, I didn't want to fuck her over. I was conflicted.

"Sasha, it's late. You're emotional. Take some time to think about it before you make a rash decision."

"Please," she said softly.

Sasha walked up to me. Our hands intertwined as she kissed me. Our kiss felt pure and loving. It felt real. I had fucked a lot of girls, but in my heart, I knew what I felt for her was stronger than what I had ever felt for anyone else that I had courted.

She led me into the bedroom, where I slowly removed her wet clothes. I waited for her to stop me as each article of clothing hit the floor. I looked at her smooth chocolate skin and knew the feelings I had for her were genuine. When I met Cheryl, I mistook fascination and adoration for love. With Sasha, the emotional connection was unlike anything I had ever experienced. It went deeper than physical attraction. She was the image of how I believed I would be if my life growing up weren't so disastrous. I envied and admired that about her at the same time.

Sasha stood in front of me, shaking. She stared at me with those big chestnut eyes as I gently glided my hands up and down her body. She started to undress me slowly. I kissed her hungrily, periodically stopping to look directly into her eyes.

"Are you sure this is what you want? You know this will change everything with us."

"You promise?" Sasha rhetorically asked, her voice shaky.

We collapsed on the bed. I stroked her face. I stopped again to search for anything in her eyes that showed a glimmer of uncertainty. Her hands quivered as she ran them up and down my thighs. I knew she was tense. I wanted to take her body to new heights and have her feeling things she couldn't fathom would be possible.

"Relax," I whispered to her.

I lowered myself down on top of her, kissed her collarbone, and sucked firmly on her neck. My eyes stayed fixed on hers. Her warm, smooth skin felt heavenly against mine. I placed my hand between her thighs. My tongue snaked around her areolas and skimmed her nipples. I spread her lips like the petals of a rose and inserted two fingers into her moistness. The combination of lapping on her nipples and massaging her vagina got her incredibly wet. I entered a third finger and moved them with a steady rhythm. I wanted her to feel my desire.

I positioned myself so that our labia were pressed firmly against each other. With her legs spread completely open, I ground my hips and rubbed her clit against mine. We held hands and enjoyed the mixture of friction and moisture. Our love felt natural. The expression on her face was euphoric. Every time I rubbed my clit against hers, I wanted her to feel the love I had for her. Seeing her excited increased the pleasure for me. Her grip on my hands became tighter. Her tempo increased. I felt my body getting close to an orgasm. I quickened my pace; then I felt the pressure building. I saw the whites of her eyes. She squirmed, and my toes curled. We climaxed together beautifully. We gasped for a moment, but I wanted more of her.

I buried my tongue into her wet peach, nibbled on her lips, and gave her quick, light flicks on the tip of her clit. Sasha gripped the top of my head, pushed my face hard into her love, and held me in place. I knew I was making love to her because I'd never felt all of my senses being satisfied with one experience. The sweet smell of her Issey Miyake perfume flooded my nostrils. The touch of her smooth skin against mine sent a shiver down my spine. Her vagina tasted like it had been dipped in honey. Hearing the loud tones of her moans and watching her look as if she were in complete bliss brought me happiness.

Afterward, I held her in my arms as she slept. My thoughts went back to when Cheryl held me after our first time having sex. This was different, though. I wouldn't hurt Sasha the way Cheryl hurt me. Not now . . . not ever.

"Did you find the answers you were looking for?" I asked.

The reality of last night hit us both. No matter what either of us said, we were more than friends now. We'd been intimate, and from the moment we made that decision, the dynamics of our relationship changed.

Tears welled up in Sasha's eyes. "I did," she said.

"What are you thinking?" I asked.

Sasha took a deep breath. Her lips trembled. She looked at me and then quickly looked down to her hands.

"I'm gay. I've known it for a while, but I've tried to suppress it. I didn't want to believe I had an attraction to women. My whole life I was taught that feelings like these were wrong."

I sat up, held her, and kissed her forehead. She wept on my chest.

"When you told me that you loved me, my heart melted. I love you too. I love everything about you, but I'm so scared. How will I explain this to my family? What will my friends think of me? Will God hate me for being gay?"

I truly felt for her. I couldn't relate to her problems because I didn't have a family to stress me about it, or a relationship with God, for that matter. My friends loved me for who I was, so this type of stress was foreign to me. Nonetheless, seeing Sasha in pain hurt me.

"Do you want to be with me?" I blurted out.

Sasha looked up at me. Her expression wore a mixture of shock and confusion.

"Yes, but . . ."

"I want to be with you too. As long as we have each other, it's you and me against the world. I'll be in your corner to help fight anything that comes your way, but I need you to do the same for me. I'm not ashamed of who I am or who I love, and if we're going to work, I need to know you'll be in my corner the same way I'm going to be there for you. Can you do that?"

"You're so much stronger than I. I wish I could be fearless like you. You're always so sure of yourself . . . so confident. I want to be with you, so I'll try my best. But you have to be patient with me. All of this is new to me."

"All of this is new to me too. I'm as scared as you are. I've never been in a committed relationship before. As long as we face everything together, I don't think we'll have anything to worry about."

"Are you sure you want to be with me? What if I can't make you happy? What if you want other women? What if you get bored with me?"

"Do you trust me?" I asked.

"Yes."

"Then believe me when I tell you that you make me happy, and I don't need anyone else. I want us to work."

We kissed and cuddled in bed. While Sasha still had a look of uncertainty on her face, her body was more relaxed. On the outside, I was cool, but inside, I was scared as shit. I was certain I loved Sasha and didn't want to lose her, so I would do whatever was necessary to make our relationship work. I was tired of chasing and turning out women. My sessions with Dr. Andrews kept replaying in my head. Sasha would not be another one of my victims. I wanted to heal and let go of the pain I held in my heart.

My relationship with Sasha would help to end that pain.

Eleven

Submissive

"Maybe this isn't such a good idea," Sasha said while placing one of her boxes on the floor of our bedroom.

Two months had passed since we decided to be official. I asked Sasha to move in with me so she could use the money she was paying for her apartment to help pay for her tuition instead. Sasha hadn't come out to her parents yet. For the time being, she told them that we were going to be roommates.

"This is a good idea. I love you, and you love me, right?"

"I love you more than anything."

"Then this is a good idea."

"What if I drive you crazy? I snore loudly, you know."

"Trust me; I've experienced it," I laughed. "I'm not worried about that. You make me better and having you around me all the time will definitely be a good thing."

I kissed her forehead.

"I'm sorry. I'm extraemotional being that it's that time. See, I'm going to be a beast already."

"You're going to be fine."

"Do you have any Midol? My cramps are killing me."

"Yeah, check the medicine cabinet in the bathroom."

Sasha walked into the bathroom. I heard the annoying creak of the cabinet opening.

Suddenly, I got a text from Jerrod. I rolled my eyes and read the message.

Jerrod: Bitch, where have you been? How many fucking nights are you gonna skip work? You realize this is your fucking job, right?

Me: I've been busy. I'll get there when I get there.

Jerrod: I'm here losing fucking money. Your fans that pay to see your stank ass every night haven't been coming around since you've been out lollygagging around.

Me: So what? Who cares?

Jerrod: Bitch, I care! This is my fucking business. Either you start coming in more or start looking for another job.

Me: Whatever, punk.

Jerrod: Bitch, try me!

I tossed my phone on my coffee table and continued with my day.

"I can't find it," Sasha called out, then paused before saying, "Um . . . Is there something you want to tell me?"

I walked to the bathroom to see what she was talking about.

"What are all these prescription bottles in here? Please don't tell me that you have an STD or something."

"Hell no! I have them because I have trouble sleeping. My doctor prescribed some sleeping pills, but I never take them."

"If they'll help you sleep better, why not?"

"My mother was a dope fiend. When I was a kid, I always saw her nodding out and being loopy. I promised myself back then that I would never be dependent on drugs for anything."

"But you drink."

"Shut up!" I laughed at her innocent comment.

"I think it's a mental thing for me. The fact that the pills are a drug makes me paranoid. I watched my mother take drugs, believing that they would take her away from her shitty existence and help her cope with her problems. Once the drugs wore off, her shitty life was still there, and it was too late to have remorse for what she had done to get the drugs. She had already sold her soul—and me, her daughter—to support her fucking drug habit. Deep down, I'm afraid of becoming addicted to any drug and turning into a fiend like my mother."

"That will never happen. You're too strong to let it happen. On top of all that, you have me. You'll never need to use anything else as a pick-me-up."

I kissed her. Sasha believed in me, supported me, and most importantly, loved me. I used to not believe in God—a part of me still questioned if He existed—but at that moment, I felt blessed.

Sasha and I walked into the club holding hands. It was only 3:00 p.m., so business was slow, but things would start to pick up around 6:00 p.m. All eyes traveled to us.

Jerrod was sitting by the bar with Sapphire and some of the bouncers. "Isis, your ass is late!" he said.

He always liked to put on a show in front of people to let it be known he was the HNIC. I brushed him off.

"The party doesn't start until I get here, so chill out and relax," I said.

"That queen shit is starting to get to your head. You ain't the Queen of Sheba in this motherfucker. You're just another dancer like all the other girls. Don't get that shit twisted."

"Yeah . . . yeah . . . yeah."

"Don't 'yeah' me. Keep it up."

"And if I keep it up, what are you going to do about it, Jerrod?"

"I don't care how many motherfuckers are lined up to see you; you keep talking shit like that, and I'll pull your ass off the stage rotation and leave you to work the floor doing table dances indefinitely."

"The only person you would be hurting is yourself if you did that. This isn't my only means of income. I do my own shit on the side, so don't get it twisted and think you have some power over me. Besides, if I'm not on the stage, how are you going to get your 10 percent?"

Jerrod sucked his teeth and mumbled under his breath. "Keep thinking you're special," he mumbled.

"Oh, I don't *think* I'm special; I *know* I am."

"You ain't shit."

"Oh yeah? That's why my posters are all over the place, right?"

"Bitch, you're good, and you got a good fan base, but don't get it twisted and think I can't replace you. Sapphire has been holding it down when you're not here. I can always put her ass on a poster and kick you to the curb. Oh, and don't think I don't see what you're doing with Sasha," he said.

Sapphire gave me a smirk and sipped on her drink.

Jerrod turned toward Sasha. "I told you this bitch was good. You were talking all that good shit about being strictly dickly and thought you couldn't become a statistic. I see she turned your ass out too."

Sasha looked embarrassed. She slowly let go of my hand.

I didn't like that she dropped my hand like that, but I understood that him saying that put her on the spot and made her uncomfortable. I let that slide . . . for the time being.

Sapphire scowled at Sasha.

"You're going to stop fucking with my money, Isis. You already fucked me by getting Jaime that job. I don't need you fucking me over again by turning out my second-string bartender and breaking her little heart. Unlike you, Sasha actually brings her ass to work. I don't have time to be hiring replacements. Fuck up again and see if I don't fire your stank ass!"

I stepped to Jerrod. There was no way in hell I was going to let him openly disrespect my girl and punk me. As soon as I was about to push him, Sasha got in the middle of us.

She looked me in my eyes. "Stop, Sammy. Just let it go. We have goals we want to accomplish. We won't be here long, but we have to make the best of this situation while we're here," she said calmly.

Sasha grabbed the sides of my face, pulled me close, and kissed me. I exhaled, relaxed my shoulders, and immediately started to calm down. I was infuriated before when Sasha let go of my hand, but kissing me in front of Jerrod helped to dampen the doubt I had, once again, only for the moment.

"Oh, cut it out. If y'all going to do that shit, do it in front of a crowd so I can make some money off that shit," Jerrod said.

I scowled at him. Sasha turned my face back to hers. "It's me and you against the world, remember? Fuck him."

"What did you say, bitch? You ain't gonna be saying fuck me in my motherfuckin' establishment."

"Yeah . . . yeah . . . yeah," she said, then raised the bar's partition, wiped off some of the shot glasses, and prepared herself for her shift.

"Don't 'yeah' me. Both of you bitches will be dancing your way on the unemployment line if you keep that shit up."

"Jerrod, sit back and enjoy the show. I'll show you why you need me here," I said confidently.

"Yeah, a'ight. You need to remember who runs shit here."

Ignoring him, I headed to the dressing room and made a post on Instagram to let my followers know I was working tonight. The only one who ran shit was me.

The DJ's voice boomed over the club's PA system, getting the crowd hyped for me.

"Fellas, this next woman needs no introduction. Get ready to crack open those wallets and get those big bills out. We have a special treat for y'all tonight. All the men want her, and all the ladies want to be her. She's the sexy, salacious, seductress," the announcer said.

I stood behind the curtain, ready to dance for the packed house.

"Get ready to adjust them cocks! Here she is . . . the one . . . the only . . . the queen of the stage . . . the Almighty Isis!"

The DJ wasted no time cueing French Montana's "Pop That." I pulled the curtain away. The spotlights were focused on the center stage. I walked out to loud applause. The whistles and catcalls made me smile. I gazed at the crowd of cheering men. A hoard of them fought to get to the front of the stage waving money in their hands. I started off dancing seductively for the crowd. I pranced around, allowing the sex-crazed men to stuff their money into my thong. Some of their fingers lingered longer than I liked, but the bouncers quickly put an end to that.

As I pulled off my black camisole, money landed rapidly onto the stage. I wouldn't pull off my G-string until I saw at least another three hundred on there. I swayed side to side, wiggling my ass in my black stilettos. I removed my G-string and dropped down into a squat with the pole between my legs. Slowly, I gyrated my hips and thrusted upward. I used to love being eye-fucked by all the faceless men. Now, I rarely looked at the crowd anymore. I didn't like to make eye contact with any of the customers after dealing with Mr. Smith. The excitement I got from dancing was fading. I was changing.

I looked over to the bar and saw Sasha working hard serving drinks. She looked at me and smiled. I gave her a wink. Seeing her helped me endure working here. She was my strength and motivation to continue making this easy money until I opened my studio. Once I did that, we both could quit this shithole.

Mr. Smith and Virginia walked into the club with Tyrone. The sight of them caused me to misstep, but I played it off seamlessly and dropped down into a split. Mr. Smith waved at me. He snapped his fingers and pointed to the spot next to him, motioning for Virginia to stand by his side. She woefully did as she was instructed, staring at the floor. Mr. Smith smiled at her meekness, pointed, and said something to her. Virginia was visibly upset and avoided eye contact with me. I focused on my routine but occasionally glanced their way.

Before long, Mr. Smith motioned for Sapphire to come to his table. She smiled and sashayed to greet him where he was sitting. She sat on his lap, and he handed her a wad of money. He threw another bundle to Tyrone. Mr. Smith and Sapphire left the table and headed toward the VIP rooms. Virginia looked pitiful and weak sitting there with her hands folded on her lap. Cinnamon came over to their table. It was obvious she saw the wad Mr. Smith tossed Tyrone and wanted a piece of that money. Tyrone sat next to Virginia grinning from ear to ear from the lap dance he splurged on Cinnamon.

My set ended to thunderous applause. Everyone stood up, high-fived, and fist pumped when I was finished. *This* was why I was the headliner. No one else got this type of response or reaction from the crowd. Jerrod sat at the bar, smiling and nodding his head. I curtsied to the crowd, bent over one last time so they could admire my luscious ass, picked up my money, and exited through the curtains to the dressing room. After changing outfits, I went to visit Sasha at the bar.

"You were great as usual," she said.

"Thanks, babe. Let me get a shot of that coconut Cîroc."

"Uh-oh, what's wrong?"

"Nothing."

"Sam, please don't lie to me. What's bothering you?"

"Mr. Smith is here with Virginia."

Sasha looked around the club.

"The white woman sitting over there with the ugly dude getting the lap dance," I told her.

"Oh . . . She's pretty. She seems really out of place here, though."

"Yeah, Mr. Smith is fucking with Sapphire now. I saw him give her money, and they headed toward the VIP rooms."

Sasha handed my shot to me. "All of that shit is behind you now. Don't sweat it."

I gave Sasha a quick peck on the lips and turned my head to see Virginia staring directly at me. She looked envious and hurt. I remember when she first came to my apartment. She was so confident and arrogant. Now, she seemed constrained and defeated. Mr. Smith returned to the table with a smile on his face. When he realized Virginia was staring at me, the smile immediately faded. I walked closer to their table to say hi to Virginia. Mr. Smith stood up.

"We're done here. Let's go!" he said.

Virginia's eyes stayed locked on mine.

"I said let's go, Virginia. Now!"

She looked down submissively. He roughly pulled her by the arm. She didn't fight or argue. She put on her coat and followed him. I felt sad for her. She wasn't strong enough to be herself. She wasn't strong enough to say, "Fuck what my family and people think." Instead, she would spend the rest of her life living a lie. I knew that could never be me.

"I don't know how you can dance all night in those heels," Sasha said.

We were sitting on the couch with my feet resting comfortably in her lap while she massaged them.

"Yeah, dancing in them all night kills my feet, but the money is worth it." I patted her hands. "Thank you, baby. It's your turn now. You work hard too. Take off your clothes and lie facedown on the sofa," I told her.

She did as she was told. I went to the room and retrieved the massage oil. I returned and knelt beside her.

I poured the oil into my hands and rubbed them together. Then I kneaded and pressed my palms all over the tense spots on her body. I used my thumbs to drive out the deep knots. Sasha looked like she was in complete bliss.

"Damn, you're going to make me go to sleep if you keep massaging me like that," she said.

"I'll have to massage another place to stir you awake, I guess."

"Can I ask you a question?"

"Sure."

"How long do you plan on working at the club?"

"Honestly, I don't know. I guess until I save enough money to open my studio. Why?"

"I'm not trying to be all in your wallet, but I think you have a lot saved already to get the ball rolling with it. All you need is a business plan, and you can get the rest of the money to start it with a loan from a bank."

I kept massaging her while thinking about my future business.

"I don't even know where to start with making a business plan. Maybe I'll just be running this shit from my apartment for the rest of my life."

"Don't talk like that. You have me, and I can help you with that."

"I don't know. What if I'm trying to get too big too fast and end up failing? I'm not going to front. I'm scared of failing."

"I've never seen you afraid of anything. You told me that this was your dream—that this was your long-term goal to get you out of that strip club. Well, babe, if this is your dream, you can't be afraid of it. You have to keep chasing it and bring it to fruition."

The passionate look in her eyes and the sincerity in her voice showed me why I loved her as much as I did.

"You're right. I'm going to woman up and work on doing this."

"You know I got your back, but promise me that if I help you run it, I'll get to quit bartending and retire from being a broke bitch."

"Deal!"

We laughed.

After that night, Sasha worked her ass off to write me a kick-ass business plan. In all, it took her about three months to get it perfect. She talked to some of her friends who studied business and got advice on what was needed to make it professional. I applied to Chase Bank for a business loan. They were impressed by my detailed business plan and the fact that I had already saved over eighty-five grand. It would be awhile until I heard anything back from them, but at least I was taking steps toward turning my dream into a reality. Having Sasha in my life only made me better.

Twelve

Rainbows and Smiles

I crept up behind Sasha and wrapped my arms around her waist. She quickly turned around, and I grabbed two big handfuls of her ass.

She looked embarrassed.

"What? I can't grab what's mine?" I said, smiling.

"What are you doing here?" Sasha asked.

"I wanted to surprise you. Why?" I asked with an attitude.

She looked at her friends. All three of them seemed confused as to who I was and why I was there on campus. She had a guilty expression on her face that let me know she never told her school friends that she was dating a woman. Sasha hated PDA. It made her feel uncomfortable when people stared at us whenever I tried to kiss her in public. Here I was trying to surprise her and pick her up from campus so she didn't have to walk home, and she was acting as if she didn't live with me.

"No reason. I know you're usually busy around this time, that's all," she said.

I looked at her skeptically.

"Aren't you going to introduce me to your friends?" I asked.

Sasha looked at me with pleading eyes as if she didn't want me to mention we were together, but I didn't give a shit. I wasn't going to live in hiding.

"Uh . . . yeah . . . guys, this is my . . . friend, Samantha," she said apprehensively.

"Friend?" I bit my lip and nodded my head. Fuck that! There was no way I would be reduced as a mere *friend*.

Sasha saw that I was pissed.

I walked closer to her friends. "Hi, I'm Sasha's girl-friend, Samantha. How are you guys doing?"

I didn't give a fuck if I embarrassed her. I told her from the start that I wasn't ashamed of who I was. I lived out loud, and there was no way I would hide in the closet with her. I shook everyone's hand, although they all gave me weak handshakes.

"Funny, Sasha's never mentioned she had a girlfriend," a white guy with square-framed glasses said.

I didn't like his judgmental tone or what he was insin-uating. Nevertheless, since they were Sasha's friends, I decided to be tactful with my response.

"Sasha is more conservative with her private life, while I'm more open and honest with mine," I replied.

I pulled Sasha to me and went in for a kiss. I swore on that moment if she pushed me away, turned for a kiss on the cheek, or made any type of negative action to-ward me, we would be through. She seemed hesitant at first but gave me a nice soft peck on the lips. Her friends looked at us in shock.

"I'll catch up with you guys tomorrow," Sasha said.

None of them said anything. They simply waved and walked away. Sasha noticed. When we got into my car, she sat quietly for a moment, bouncing her legs rapidly in frustration.

"Why did you do that?" she groaned and placed her palm on her forehead.

"Why wouldn't I? We're dating, aren't we? You're not ashamed to be with me, right?"

"I'm not, but I didn't come out to them yet. I wanted to do it at the right time, and you outed me before I was ready. Some of them know my family. What if they say something?"

"If they do, it'll give your family time to digest it before you tell them officially."

"No, Sam, that's *not* how it works. You embarrassed me in front of them. Again, I wanted to do it when the time was right."

"So, what do you expect me to do? Am I supposed to twiddle my thumbs and wait until you finish dragging your feet? When you decided to be with me, you decided that this was what you wanted. Don't break your word now and hide it from the world. Be proud of what and who you are. There is nothing to be ashamed of."

Sasha looked at me with piercing eyes. "You know what? Let's drop it."

I let it go because I was already upset, and I knew myself. If I kept arguing with her, I would eventually say something that I would regret. While we put the battle on hold, I knew this war was only beginning.

Two months passed, and I still hadn't heard anything from the bank regarding my business loan. I started to think it was a bad sign, and I would never get approved. Lately, I had been depressed and irritable. I felt like I would be trapped stripping into old age.

Sasha was the only thing keeping my dream alive. She regularly advertised for me on campus and handled my website. Her optimistic, upbeat attitude was the only positive glimmer of hope that everything would be okay, and I would fulfill my dream. I realized having Sasha in my life and talking to Dr. Andrews took the place of the attention and rush that being onstage gave me. Lately, when I stepped on the stage, I felt emptier with each performance. Seeing Virginia and Mr. Smith that night had further driven the point that I wanted to get out of the business, and I knew the only way out would be with my studio. However, not hearing from the bank was driving me crazy and causing me to snap at everyone.

As always, my girls, Jaime and Silka, knew the best way to cheer me up from my shitty attitude was to hang out in the village. Saturday night, we barhopped. We were walking around West Fourth Street and Avenue of the Americas laughing and having a good time when a caramel-colored brother with wavy hair bumped into me. I could have sworn someone smacked my ass and let their hand linger. It felt more like a grope than an accident. I was ready to flip out and smack the shit out of whoever it was that did it.

"*Excuse* you. Watch where you're going and keep your paws to yourself," I barked.

"Oops! Sorry about that," the brother said.

He stood there smiling with his three friends. All of them looked like they were up to no good.

"Yo, you bitches are bad! Why don't you and your friends hang out with us? We can—" He stopped midsentence and pointed at his black Nike shirt with the words *Just Do It* in red lettering. I frowned at him and looked him up and down.

"Just do it, huh? I'd rather not. You're not my type," I said, then lifted Sasha's hand to show him that I was holding it.

He nudged his friends with a sly smile. "Oh, I get it. These bitches are rug munchers!"

"Fuck you, asshole! It's niggas like you that make me proud to be a lesbian," I shot back, with a frown etched on my face.

"Watch your mouth, dickhead!" Jaime said.

Silka tried to calm us down as a crowd started forming around us. The guy looked at Sasha, who was uncomfortable with the attention this altercation brought us.

"Can we just go?" Sasha asked.

We tried to walk away, but the caramel brother blocked our path. I've dealt with his type before. He believed that being a lesbian was a choice, and if he said the right things and fucked us the right way, he could "convert" us to being straight. Guys like him wouldn't stop until he was embarrassed. If that's what it would take for him to leave us alone, I was going to embarrass the shit out of him.

He looked Sasha up and down. He circled us and licked his lips. "What's the matter, baby? You couldn't find a guy that was man enough to please you?" he said, as he grabbed his crotch and stared at her.

Sasha's eyes got dark, and her nostrils flared. I knew his comment pissed her off because I remembered how angry she was when her ex made a similar comment.

"She's not interested, and from what I just saw you grab, you don't have nothing that could sway her anyway," I said smugly.

Everyone, including his friends, laughed at my remark. He looked humiliated.

"Fuck you, you stupid dyke bitch!"

"I see you have a short memory to go with your short dick. I'm a *lesbian,* remember? I'm not going to fuck you."

Everyone laughed harder at my jokes. The crowd pointed at us. With every snicker and sneer, Sasha became more introverted. She let go of my hand, placing her hands in her jean pockets.

That hurt me. I felt as if she were embarrassed by our relationship.

The caramel guy pushed me. "Shut up, you stupid lesbo!" He scowled at me with his fist balled.

"Wow, you're quick. How long did it take you to come up with that? Also, you do realize that calling a lesbian a lesbo isn't an insult, right? Stay in school, buddy." There was more laughter.

"Babe, that's enough. Please, let's get out of here," Sasha said, pleading with me to leave.

The guy shoved me again—this time, a lot rougher.

"Leave her alone," a random gay white man said as he passed, holding the hand of his black lover.

"Oh, look, the fags are sticking up for the fag."

"Yeah, keep spewing your hate talk. The ones that hate us the most are usually the main ones in my inbox on the low, asking if they can suck me," the gay white man shot back. Again, there was more laughter from the crowd.

"Yeah, right. I wouldn't be caught dead touching one of you faggots."

The more he went on, the more Sasha went in to herself. I was embarrassed by the way she was acting. Seeing her like that made me emotional; I couldn't control myself. I pushed him back after hearing his continued insults. He punched me in the nose. I scratched his face. His friends stopped Jaime and Silka from coming to my aid. I defiantly stood my ground, preparing myself for whatever happened next.

"Come on, bitch. You wanna act like a man, I'm gonna fuck you up like one," he said.

I dashed toward him. I felt a swift right hook connect to the side of my head next to my temple. The blow hit me so hard that I lost my balance, and my knees gave out. My body plummeted to the pavement. I picked myself up and charged at him again. He kicked me in the stomach, causing me to gasp for air. I collapsed to the concrete clutching my stomach and coughing. He kicked me in the face, then continued to kick and stomp on me. I balled myself up, blocking my face with my forearms. Quickly, I glanced through the folds of my arms to see his friends stopping anyone who tried to save me from this beating. Those who weren't trying to help videotaped the whole thing with their phones and cheered at my drama. Sasha cried as he continued his assault. I heard sirens in the distance.

"Come on, nigga! Let's go! I ain't getting locked up over you beating up some dyke bitch," one of his friends said.

I lay on the street bloodied and bruised. Silka and Jaime hurriedly picked me up off the ground.

"Oh my God! Sam, are you okay?" Silka asked, as she held my chin and turned my head. She attempted to dust me off gently. Her eyes roved up and down my body, checking for visible injuries.

"I can't believe these fucking savages!" Jaime said. She yelled at them as they ran around the corner. "I bet you feel real big beating up a fucking woman. Now, look at y'all running like fucking pussies. You cowards!"

Two cops quickly exited their car—a Hispanic officer and a brother. Silka ran toward them and explained what went down. I heard the Hispanic officer radio in to the dispatcher the three guys' descriptions. Jaime tried her best to gather napkins and paper towels from the stores on the block to clean up my bloody face. Sasha held my hand while I talked with the cops.

"Ma'am, you should go to the hospital. We can send you to Bellevue if you would like," the Hispanic officer suggested.

I looked at Sasha. Tears streamed down her face. She shook her head and held herself.

"Nah, I'm not going to the hospital. I just want to go home."

"Ma'am, your injuries look pretty bad. You should seriously get checked out," the black officer said.

"I'm fine," I replied firmly.

The officers wanted to take a report. They wanted to label it as a hate crime, but I declined. We didn't know the guys' names, addresses, or any other information that would lead to them getting caught, so I didn't feel like going through the aggravation. What hurt more than the ass beating was feeling betrayed by Sasha. I felt like when the shit hit the fan, she wasn't secure enough to claim me as the one she was with. While I was proud to have her on my arm, she folded and was embarrassed by me in the face of adversity. It made me believe she'd become another closet case, and I had no room in my life for hasbians.

We walked slowly to my Jeep. Jaime drove since I was in no shape to get behind the wheel. Sasha sat quietly in a daze. She had tears in her eyes as she looked out of the rear passenger window.

"I already talked to Dom. When we get to your place, he's going to take a look at you," Silka said.

"I don't want him touching me. I'm fine."

"Stop being so damn hardheaded. That guy almost killed you. I'm not taking no for an answer. You're my sister, and I'm going to help you."

While I hated her being pushy, the fact that she was so concerned made me happy.

"You should've reported those assholes," Jaime said, shaking her head.

"Why? They would've never caught them anyway. It's not like anyone watching would've given the cops their cell phone videos. The cops already put the description of the guys over the radio minutes after it happened and found nothing. Those guys were already long gone. By the end of the night, footage of me getting my ass beat will get a million hits on YouTube."

"What kind of man would beat on a fucking woman like that?" Jaime asked angrily.

"A man that's intimidated by one," I told her.

When we arrived at my apartment building, Dom was waiting in a parking spot across the street with a big medical bag in one hand and a car seat holding the baby in the other. Silka swiftly walked over to him and grabbed the car seat.

"Hey, honey! She wouldn't go to the hospital. Please try to talk some sense into her."

I rolled my eyes as Dom kissed Silka softly. Once we entered my apartment, Dom and I went to my bedroom. Everyone else hung out in the living room.

"Give me a minute. I want to clean myself up," I said.

Dom nodded. I got some clothes out of my dresser and threw the TV remote to him. He caught it and flicked through the channels, settling on watching the movie *Fight Club*.

In my bathroom, I looked at my reflection in the mirror and wanted to cry. I removed my bloody clothes, turned on the shower, adjusted the temperature of the water until it was almost too hot to handle, and then stepped inside. I stood directly under the showerhead, allowing the water to flow down my body. The water mixed with my blood and tears. I winced as the loofah grazed over the raised purple welts on my body. The knot on my head pulsated heavily. My arms, sides, and legs were covered in bruises and small cuts.

While the world had made great strides, there was still hatred toward gays. The majority of people will never understand that love is love, and we cannot change why we are the way we are. This lifestyle isn't a choice. We cannot change who we're attracted to. While I had my doubts about God, I prayed that one day all of the hatred toward us would stop.

I finished showering and changed into leggings and a T-shirt. Dom tried to be as gentle as he could while examining me, but I grimaced with every touch. He poured some peroxide on a cloth and dabbed the back of my head and face.

"Well, the good news is you don't have any broken bones. The bad news is you have a lot of little scrapes and bruises. I'd relax for a few days. Continue to apply ice packs to your bruises, and here's some Bacitracin to put on the scrapes," Dom said.

As much shit as I put him through, he always remained calm, was never disrespectful, and didn't fight back with me.

"Can I ask you something?" I said.

"Sure, what's up?"

"You never say shit about me being a lesbian, Silka hanging out with me at gay clubs, or fight back when

I make fun of you for being white. Why? Deep down, doesn't it bother you that I'm so close to her?"

He smiled. "No, because first, I'm secure. I know Silka loves me and wouldn't do anything to hurt me or betray my trust. Second, I don't hate that you're a lesbian. Silka loves you. You're family to her. If you mean that much to her, and she sees you like a sister, then I'll see you the same way because I love her. I would never hate you for being gay because I understand what it feels like to be discriminated against."

"What nonsense are you talking about, white man?"

He laughed. "Seriously, I've always been attracted to women of color. When you're in interracial relationships, people treat you badly most times. Your family may treat you differently, and there are a lot of close minded people out there. The same way I want people to respect my relationship with Silka is the same way I treat you with being gay. I don't have to agree with it, nor do I have to like it, but as a human being, I respect it."

I nodded.

"Do you only like her because she's black?" I asked bluntly.

"I can't help what I'm attracted to any more than you can, but my love for Silka goes deeper than her skin color. She's loving, driven, outgoing, and above all else, she makes me better and keeps me happy."

"All right . . . Don't get all mushy on me."

He chuckled. "Am I still your least favorite white boy?"

"Always," I chuckled.

For the first time ever, we fist bumped and smiled together. Then we walked into the living room laughing. After talking to Dom, I trusted and respected him more. I would ease up on teasing him . . . or at least I would try.

Silka and Jaime were sitting on the couch playing with the baby, while Sasha flipped through channels on the TV.

"Good news, everyone! Samantha took a licking, but she'll keep on ticking."

Silka punched him in the arm. "Poor choice of words, babe."

"What? Licking?"

Jaime laughed. Silka playfully punched him again.

"Seriously, though, she's all good. She's a little bruised up, but nothing that ice and a little rest can't fix."

"After tonight's excitement, I'm going to head home and relax a little myself. Hit me up if you need anything," Jaime said.

"Yeah, we're going to head out too. I haven't spent any time with Dom or the baby today."

When they left, I confronted Sasha. "What was up with you today?" I asked.

"What do you mean?"

"You acted all weird when those assholes approached us. You let go of my hand and acted like you weren't with me. What's up with that?"

"I . . . I don't know if I can do this."

"Oh, don't give me this shit now. Don't flip-flop just because everything isn't all rainbows and smiles."

"I don't know if I'm ready for all of that yet. I was terrified by them. They embarrassed us."

"Embarrassed *us* or embarrassed *you?* I wasn't embarrassed. You think this is the first time I had to fight a dude who had a problem with me being a lez? Not even close. I've fought lots of guys; I don't give a fuck who it is. I'll fight anybody who has a problem with my lifestyle. I didn't care if they saw me with you. I was proud to stand next to you, and I expect the same from you. If someone made fun of you being black and attacked you, would you be ashamed, cower in fear, and run away . . . or would you fight and stand up for yourself?"

"That's not the same thing."

"It *is* the same thing."

"I'm not as strong as you, okay? I don't like having all of that attention. This isn't the same thing as being black."

"It's not? I can't help being gay just like I can't help being black. It's not a fucking choice! If you can't see that by now, then what are we doing? The same way you're proud to be black, you should be proud to be a lesbian—not ashamed of it."

"I don't like negative attention. I don't like people gawking at me like I'm some weirdo."

"Is that what you feel you are?"

"No, I'm not saying that. I don't know what I'm saying."

"Have you told your parents that you're dating me yet?"

She looked down at the carpet.

"I knew it. You just want to stay in the closet. Well, I got news for you, honey. I'm done dealing with closet cases."

This is what happens when I try to change. I get brought back to reality, I thought. I felt foolish for thinking a relationship with Sasha would work.

She didn't say a word. She cried and stared down at the carpet.

"I listened to you bullshit me and lying, saying that you love me. If you love someone, you're not ashamed to be with them. If you love someone, you don't hide it from your family. You know what? Get out! Leave! Don't talk

to me, don't apologize, and forget that you know me." I
threw my hands up in disgust.

"I have no place else to go. All of my stuff is here.
What am I supposed to do?" she cried.

"I don't give a shit. Get out! Wherever you end up, I'll
have your shit sent to you."

Sasha started bawling as she slowly picked up her
purse and headed for the door. I held the door open and
slammed it shut behind her. I placed my back against the
door and slid down to the floor; then I cupped my face
in my hands. Between my aches and pains, worrying
about my business loan, and my anger with Sasha, I was
emotionally drained.

I heard a faint knock on my door. I knew it was Sasha.
I knew she probably came back to apologize. I wanted
to stay mad at her. I wanted to hate her, but I loved her.
I slowly rose from the floor and opened the door. Sasha
stood in front of me in tears, wringing her hands.

"I'm sorry," she said.

"It's okay, but this can't work if you're not going to
claim me."

"Can you help me tell my parents?"

I smiled at her and nodded. I knew this would be
difficult for her, but I would be there to help her battle
through it.

"You okay over there?" I asked.

"I'm so fucking nervous. I don't know how they're
going to react. I keep playing it out in my head, and every
version turns out fucked up."

We drove to Sasha's parents' house. It had been two
months, but she decided that her birthday, September

22nd, would be the day to come out to her parents. Sasha had been quiet the entire ride. I worried about her. I knew this wouldn't be easy for her religious family to digest. I never had to come out to anyone. A part of me felt guilty and selfish. I knew she loved me, but she was very close to her family. I didn't want her to lose them because of me. I hoped we could get them to accept our love and make this a smooth transition.

I parked my car in front of the house. Sasha was shaking. She blew out air, tilted her head back, and stared at the roof of my vehicle.

"Are you okay? Do you still want to go through with this today, or do you want to wait?"

Sasha shook her head. "No. If I don't do this now, I'll never do it."

I patted her hand and gave her a warm smile. "It's me and you against the world. You know I got your back. Everything will be fine," I assured her.

Sasha's mother came out of the house to greet us. "How are you girls doing?"

"I'm fine, Momma."

"I'm good, Mrs. Small."

"I made macaroni and cheese, mashed potatoes, and ribs. We're going to eat good tonight," Mrs. Small said.

"I can't wait, Momma," Sasha responded halfheartedly.

"Chile, why you got on that face?" Mrs. Small asked.

"I need to tell the family something important. Can you have everyone come into the living room?"

Mrs. Small started to panic. "Oh my goodness, is everything okay? You're not pregnant, are you?"

"No, no . . . Nothing like that."

"What is it then?"

"Momma, come on. Get everyone to come to the living room. I'll tell everyone once we're all together."

"Okay, okay . . . I'm on it."

Mrs. Small walked toward the stairs and yelled for everyone to come down.

"All right, y'all stop what you're doing and listen up. Sasha's here and wants to talk to everyone. Jimmy, Joseph, cut that TV off. Poppa, quit trying to fix that dishwasher and come here in the living room. I guess you all will be helping me wash the dishes by hand tonight. Josephine, hang up that telephone. You're not paying the bill here."

Everyone gradually did what they were told. They sat down on the couch in the living room, while Sasha stood in the center of the floor. I stood firmly next to her. All of their eyes were on her. Sasha had goose bumps. I touched her shoulder and held her hand. Mrs. Small had a confused look on her face.

"All right, chile, you got our undivided attention. What is it exactly that you have to tell us?" Mrs. Small asked.

Sasha turned around and covered her face. She looked up at me.

"I can't do this."

"I know it's hard, but if you don't get it off your chest, you'll always be living in hiding," I said.

She nodded and faced them again.

"Momma . . . Poppa . . . I've always had these feelings that I couldn't explain. No matter what guy I was with . . . I always felt something was missing with them. I never felt whole."

"What are you saying, Sasha?" Reverend Small asked sternly.

"Sasha, are you telling us that you're a lesbian?" Josephine asked.

Sasha's eyes became teary, and she nodded. Taking a deep breath, she looked at me, grabbed my hand, and faced her parents.

"I'm in love with Samantha. She's more than just a friend. She's my girlfriend. I'm a lesbian."

Sasha's father threw his hands in the air. Mrs. Small's hand clutched her chest like she was going to have a heart attack. Her siblings looked at one another in shock.

"No, you're not. I didn't raise no damn dyke. This . . . this . . . is just a phase. You're young and confused, and this hussy is the cause of it." Mrs. Small looked me up and down in disgust.

"No, Momma, I've always felt this way. I've tried to suppress it, but I can't. This is who I am."

"No child of mine is going to be a homosexual," Reverend Small shouted, his voice so deep and powerful that it made me flutter. "We took you to church every Sunday. We raised you right. You *know* better than this."

"I'm so disappointed in you, Sasha. You know God doesn't approve of gays. He hates them. 'Thou shalt not lie with mankind as with womankind. It is an abomination,' Leviticus 18:22," Mrs. Small said.

"You always taught me that God was a God of love and not hate. You taught me that God loves all His children. And we have known and believed the love that God hath to us. God is love; and he that dwelleth in love dwelleth in God, and God in him, 1 John 4:16."

Reverend Small walked up to Sasha and smacked her forcefully. "How dare you bend the Word of God to promote your . . . your . . . filthy lifestyle," he said.

Sasha's eyes welled with tears. Her siblings looked away, acting as if she were nothing to them. I reached for her, but she waved me away.

"It's okay, Sam. My father is always talking about the truth, but he can't take it when someone speaks the truth right back to him."

"You're not going to disrespect me in this house."

"You're a sinner too, Poppa. 'He that is without sin among you, let him first cast a stone at her,' John 8:7. You slept with lots of women in our congregation, and you continue to do it. What makes your sins any less than mine? 'For whoever keeps the whole law and yet stumbles at just one point is guilty of breaking all of it,' James 2:10. You taught me that, Poppa."

"How dare you?" Reverend Small went to hit Sasha again, but I stepped in front of her.

"You're too close minded to see that you're wrong. She's trying to help you understand, and instead of listening to her, you become primitive and beat on her."

As soon as those words left my lips, Reverend Small punched and started to choke me.

"You fucking bitch! This is all *your* fault. You *ruined* my baby. She was fine until *you* came into her life and contaminated her head."

He wrapped his rough hands tightly around my neck; his thumbs pressed against my larynx, constricting my breathing. My eyes watered as the room blurred. I couldn't breathe. I tried to claw and pry his hands open, but his strength was too much for me. I began to lose conscious. Sasha jumped on his back and commenced to hitting him. He let go of me. I gasped for air and crawled away from him. Sasha scratched his face. His eyes widened. He touched the scratched area and saw blood on his fingertips. Mrs. Small grabbed him before he got to Sasha. She shook her head while staring at him. Speechless, Sasha's siblings stood there with their mouths wide open.

Mrs. Small walked up to Sasha. "You're an embarrassment to your family, to God, and to yourself. From this day forward, we no longer consider you our child. You're *dead* to us. You disobeyed one of the most important commandments—honor thy father and thy mother. You disrespected us by bringing this harlot into our home, and you blatantly twisted the Word of God when you know we taught you the correct meaning of it. You disgust me."

She slapped Sasha hard across the face. Mrs. Small covered her mouth to hold in her whimpers as her eyes filled with tears.

Sasha's lips trembled. "Mama, please . . ." Mrs. Small turned her back on her.

"Josephine, can you talk to them, please?" Sasha begged.

Josephine mimicked her mother's actions.

"Jimmy . . . Joseph . . . You'll talk to them for me, right?"

They looked like they wanted to say something, but instead, they looked away and acted as if they couldn't hear her. Mrs. Small handed the reverend some tissues for his face.

While holding the tissues firmly against the scratched area on his face, he said, "Get out of here. As of now, you are no longer our daughter. Go back to your den of sin and stay there."

"Don't say that, Daddy. I love you guys."

"We loved you too, but the day you decided to be with this . . . this . . . woman, you stopped being our daughter. You're *dead* to us now."

"Don't say that, Daddy. Please!"

"Get out!" Reverend Small shouted.

"Daddy, no! Don't do this!"

"I'm not your daddy. Get out of this house."

"Mama, say something, please!"

"Leave! You broke my heart today. I can't take any more of this," Mrs. Small replied, then grabbed Sasha by the arm, opened the door, and pushed her out.

Sasha went flying off the stoop and skinned her knees when she hit the pavement. As I ran after her and picked her up off the ground, Reverend Small shut the door behind us.

Sasha was broken. She cried hysterically and reached for the door. Seeing her cry so hard made me cry, but I had to pry her away from the door.

"Baby, let's go. It's pointless right now to say anything else to your parents. Our best bet is to let things cool down and try to talk to them once they calm down."

Sasha nodded.

I walked her to my Jeep, rested her head on my shoulder, and let her cry. My heart was broken. If they weren't going to be her family, fuck them. We'd be our own family.

I sat in a daze in front of the mirror, applying my makeup. I felt drained emotionally. I didn't want to be there, but there I was, sitting at a vanity table in the strip club's locker room putting on my eyeliner.

It had been two months since Sasha came out to her family, and they had been extremely hard on her—changing the locks to the house in addition to changing their cell and house numbers. Her friends from her college had distanced themselves from her once she confirmed she was officially dating a woman. I treaded lightly around Sasha. I felt responsible for her fucked-up family life and her school friends giving her the cold shoulder, but I didn't know how to fix things.

Sasha cried a lot. She barely ate, hardly slept, and I was having trouble reaching her. She missed her family badly, and the fact that they cut her off pained her every day. She had been withdrawn from me lately, and I felt lonely. Since she has been like this, we hadn't gone anywhere fun as a couple. We hadn't joked around or done anything to strengthen our bond. She hadn't fucked me, and we didn't have those in-depth conversations like we used to. I bought her a new car and other gifts, hoping they would cheer her up, but nothing I did or said broke her out of her depression. A part of me felt guilty. I felt like maybe I rushed her into this life or didn't prepare her enough for how certain people would react to her being honest about her sexuality.

To make matters worse, my dreams had been fucking with me hardcore lately. Usually, Sasha would calm me down and ease me through them, but she had been so wrapped up in her own shit that she left me to calm myself down. The times when she did sleep, she slept through my fits.

"What are you thinking about so hard?" Sapphire asked.

"Nothing," I said, sucking my teeth.

"It has to be something. You've been staring at the wall for twenty minutes."

I ignored her, but she wouldn't let it go.

"You look like your mind is a million miles away. Were you daydreaming about the last time we fucked?" she joked.

This trick had to be buggin'. I didn't give a shit about her.

Sapphire walked up to me and wrapped her arms around my waist. She was hot, but she was too clingy and possessive. Fucking her always got her in her feelings, and it wasn't worth the headache. I could only take her in small doses.

"I'm going through a lot of shit right now," I told her while removing her arms from around me.

"Where's your girl tonight?"

"She's on campus at the library working on one of her term papers."

"Oh, that's too bad. I know if my boo were stressed out, I couldn't concentrate on work until she was satisfied."

"Is that right?"

"Yep, what do you see in her anyway? I mean, she's cute, but why have cute when you can have *this*?" Sapphire pointed to her body.

"I love her."

"You love her, huh? I don't see her sporting any jewelry. I still wear the earrings that you bought me every day. I cherish them. They *always* remind me of you." She tugged on her ears.

She was referring to the diamond-studded earrings I bought her when I was trying to tap that. She wasn't even a challenge. Once I wined and dined her, bought her a couple of gifts, and got in her head, it didn't take long to turn her out easily. Sasha, on the other hand, was never into the materialistic bullshit. So, I never bought her expensive jewelry. She would rather I spend that money on something we could do together than spend it on some shiny metal.

"Why do you always flirt with me so hard, especially when you know I have a girl?" I asked.

"That didn't stop you from stepping to me when I had a man. I want the same thing you want."

"And what's that?"

"To fuck!"

"Nah, I'm good. Look, I'm sure there are other women out there that would love to fuck your brains out, but—"

"I don't want them to fuck me. I want *you*. I've lost all interest in men. I've been with other women after you, but they are no comparison. I know you're not going to leave Sasha for me, but that doesn't mean we can't still have fun."

"I . . . I couldn't do that to her."

"Come on. Please. Don't make me beg. I'm offering this good pussy to you. I hated the way things ended with us. Can you at least give me one last time?"

I felt my heart screaming at my brain to tell her no. I wanted to resist, but I felt my will weakening.

"The club is dead as fuck tonight. Since you haven't been working here as much, the crowd has been getting smaller, and Jerrod's been having a fit." Sapphire giggled. "It's early. Let go of some of that stress and fuck me."

"All right, fuck it! Where you want to do this?"

"Can we go to your place?"

It was one thing to fuck around on Sasha; it was another to do it in the bed we shared.

"Nah, let's go to your place."

"I would have said let's go there, but I have family in from out of town, and my place is a wreck. Let's just go to your place. I promise I'll be out before your girl gets home."

I thought against it, but my strap and toys were at my place, and I wanted to wear this bitch out. Before I knew it, I was walking into my apartment with Sapphire, who followed me in her car since I didn't want to drive back to the club afterward and feel everyone's eyes looking at me for cheating. I felt like my body was moving in automatic. I hadn't missed fucking random women. Yet, I was reverting back to that bad habit.

Sapphire kissed me on the lips while we took each other's clothes off.

"My body has been craving this for so long. I need this," she whispered in my ear.

Our kisses felt empty to me. That energy I felt whenever I touched Sasha was missing when I kissed Sapphire.

I pushed her onto the bed and told her. "Don't move. Stay right there."

I went to my dresser drawer, retrieved my strap, put it on, and stared at Sapphire. With her back flat on the bed, she swayed her thighs from side to side, ready for me to take her. I wanted to stop myself, but I needed something to distract me from my problems. Fucking Sapphire would be that temporary fix I needed to numb myself and shut my mind down so I wouldn't feel the loneliness of Sasha not being intimate with me lately, or thinking about when I'd see her moping around depressed. My biggest concern, fear, was that she regretted being a lesbian and would eventually leave me.

I forcefully pushed Sapphire's legs open. She held them all the way back to the point where the bottoms of her feet were touching my headboard. I rammed my dildo inside of her until I couldn't fit any more of it in her. She wrapped her arms around my neck and pulled me closer to her.

"Aaah, oooh . . . I missed this so much, baby. Fuck me!"
"Shut up!" I yelled.

Memories of my childhood, the countless men who had raped me, and my experiences with Mr. Smith hit me all at once. I felt no better than those assholes and fucking pedophiles that used to touch me.

"Damn, baby! You're shaking. Are you about to come so soon?" she asked.

Far from it, I thought, feeling really emotional. My eyes began to swell with tears. I buried my face between her breasts and licked the sides of them to hide my face. I pounded her ferociously.

"Oh God! That's it . . . I'm going to come!"

I felt like a drug fiend who had relapsed. Memories of my mother crept into my head. I heard the voice of Dr. Andrews. *You substitute drugs with a different addiction—women. I know you care about Sasha, and I know she cares about you. Don't let that addiction push her away . . .*

I gasped and pulled out of Sapphire.

"Damn, baby, you've never been this intense."

I pushed her back down on the bed, fingering her and licking her clit to hide the pain on my face.

After watching her get off numerous times, I excused myself and went into my bathroom. I grabbed a towel and fell to the floor, sobbing into the towel to muffle my cries. I gathered myself to kick this bitch out before Sasha got home. Taking a deep breath, I turned the knob to the bathroom door. What I thought would help my stress only left me full of regret and hating myself.

"Shit, baby, it's not what you think."

Sasha stood motionless staring at our bed. Sapphire, who was still naked under the cover, was smiling. Sasha collapsed to the floor and burst into tears.

"How is this *not* what I think? I . . . I . . . couldn't concentrate on shit for my paper. So, I came home to be with you . . . and *this* is what I find? You fucking this bitch in *our* bed?"

"Who you callin' a bitch, bitch?" Sapphire fired back.

Sasha rushed toward her, grabbed Sapphire by her hair, and started delivering punches to her face. I grabbed Sasha. She kicked, clawed, and screamed in an attempt to get back at Sapphire. Finally, she stopped fighting me and dropped back down to her knees. Sapphire pulled the comforter off and threw it to the floor.

"Keep your bitch on a leash! Tell me, what does *she* got that *I* don't got, huh? Why do I get some fucking earrings while she gets the *real* prize—you? I poured my heart out to you. I would've done anything for you, so why *her?*"

"Fuck it! You can have her," Sasha said.

"No, wait! I'm so sorry. She meant nothing to me . . . really! It was just sex, nothing more. I was lonely and vulnerable. I wasn't thinking." I pleaded with Sasha for forgiveness.

"I meant nothing? Fuck you, Samantha!" Sapphire took off her earrings and threw them at Sasha. "I don't need anything from this bitch. All she does is use women up and spit them out."

Sapphire turned to me. "I've wanted you and waited for you all this time, hoping that one day, things would be different, and you would see me as more than a jump-off, but I guess that wasn't in the cards for you and me."

She turned to face Sasha. "Look, don't be stupid like I've been. Samantha doesn't give a fuck about anyone but herself!"

Sapphire quickly put on her clothes, ran out of my bedroom, and slammed the apartment door shut on her way out.

Sasha picked herself up from off the floor and looked at me. I couldn't look her in the eyes.

"How could you do this to me?" she asked.

"Sasha, I love you. I—"

I took a step toward her and reached for her. She pulled away and took steps backward.

"Don't . . . Don't you dare use love in any sentence you say to me. I *loved* you. I loved you so much that I sacrificed everything to be with you. Why? Help me understand why you did this to me."

Her eyes scanned my face like they were searching for answers to questions I wasn't sure I could give her right away. There wasn't exactly one specific reason why I did it. She deserved some explanation, but I couldn't fix my mouth to tell her some bullshit. There was nothing I could say to justify what I did.

"I honestly don't know how to answer that. I was just being stupid and emotional and—"

"Don't fucking lie to me! Tell me the fucking truth!"

She was right. Shit just got real, so it was time to be up front and honest.

"You want the truth? Okay, here it is. You've been moping around so much that I felt neglected. Instead of talking to me and sharing your pain so we could get over it together, you shut me out. I was lonely. I was scared of how the future would turn out for us. I missed our intimacy. My nightmares were bothering me. I felt like you regretted being with me, and I needed you."

"Are you fucking serious? You sound really selfish right now. My friends look at me like I'm some fucking leper. My family disowned me, and you're only thinking of yourself. You only give a shit about *your* needs. It's not always about you. I've always been there for you. I've always supported you. I *needed* support!"

"I've tried to support you. I couldn't reach you. You were distant—"

"You should've tried harder. Not fucking *cheat* on me."

"Why can't you just get over it?"

"Get over my family or the fact you fucked another girl in our bed? You have no idea what I'm going through. You never had a family to lose. Your friends never abandoned you."

Sasha bringing up that I didn't have a family stung me. It felt like a deliberate slap in my face.

"Oh well, put on your big-girl panties and deal with it. You having this 'woe is me' attitude doesn't help anyone," I told her.

"You know, you can be so cold sometimes. You hate men, but you're worse than they are. You know why this hurts worse than being cheated on by a man? Because you're a *woman*. You *know* better. When a man hurts a woman, he may fuck with their head to get some ass, but it's sort of expected. You're deeply rooted in my heart. You understand women because you are one. So, when you hurt me, it's a million times worse."

"Stop being so dramatic. You walk around like someone died."

"If I walk around like someone died, it's because you're dead inside. You promised me that you would never hurt me, and you reneged on that promise. You tell me that I should just *get over* losing everything important to me and let it go, but do you know why you keep having your nightmares? *You* can't let shit go. Don't tell me how I should act and feel when you're the same way," Sasha said.

That hurt. What she said was the truth and something I never wanted to acknowledge. I wanted to scream. I felt my blood boiling and my hands shaking. I understood her anger, and I truly regretted cheating on her, but her words pissed me off, and I wanted to hurt her with the same ferocity that I felt.

"If you're going to act dead, then you should just die!"

Sasha's mouth dropped open in shock. I couldn't believe those words left my mouth. I blurted it out before I had a chance to think about the severity of what I was saying. I didn't mean it, but when I was angry, I said a lot of shit I didn't mean. Sasha ran out of the bedroom. I followed after her.

"Sasha, wait!"

"No, fuck you! Leave me alone!"

She ran out of the apartment, leaving the door wide open. I rushed back to my bedroom and grabbed my clothes. I stumbled and fumbled to get dressed while chasing after her. She ran to her car, jumped in, started it, and sped off.

I rushed to my car to follow her. I sped, zipping through traffic. Sasha weaved in and out of lanes. Chasing after her had me running red lights, racing through stop signs, dodging people crossing the street, and cutting cars off, trying my hardest to catch up to her. Drivers were honking at us and yelling out of their car windows. Those who were walking gave us the finger. Only one car separated me from being directly behind her. The traffic light turned yellow. The car in front of me slowed to a stop while Sasha sped on. I got caught at the light.

***

I drove for what felt like an eternity looking for Sasha. I searched everywhere. I felt like all hope was lost until I got a call from an unfamiliar number. I answered, and it was Sasha's sister, Josephine.

"Hello?" I answered.

"Yeah, you need to come to my parents' house and get this girl before she causes my parents any more grief."

"Sasha's at your parents' house?"

"Yes, and they would appreciate it if you got her and left. She's embarrassed them enough, and when she decided to be a lesbian, she was made aware that by choosing that lifestyle, she would be shunned by God and her family for good because of her perversion. So, *come and get her*."

"How can you be so fucking cold and heartless and speak about your sister like that?"

"When she chose to be with you, she stopped being my sister."

Her statement made me hate religion even more. I hated that it could control people so much they would reject their own flesh and blood over an interpretation of words.

"I'm on my way," I said.

Josephine hung up.

I pulled up to Sasha's parents' house. Their door was open. I walked in to the sight of Sasha on her knees, crying and groveling at her father's feet.

"Daddy, please don't say that," Sasha begged.

"No, you're no longer a part of this family," he said firmly. Reverend Small looked up at me. "And *you* . . . Get her out of here. You had her at your home living in sin? She is *your* responsibility now."

Sasha's mother sat on the sofa, crying silently as her daughter pleaded with her father.

"Daddy, I'm still that little girl you raised. I'm still that little girl you played with and taught how to ride a bike. The fact that I'm in love with a woman doesn't change anything."

"It changes *everything*. You have embarrassed us enough. Leave!" Reverend Small faced me. His eyes tightened, and his teeth clenched.

"Do you see what you did? My little girl, my firstborn, is gone from me forever because of *you*. *You* did this. She knew what the consequences would be if she chose you over God and her family, and *you* hurt her. She has to live with her choice now, and we have to live with ours. Nothing will alter my decision."

Sasha crawled over to her mother. "Momma, please . . . Talk to him. He'll listen if you talk to him."

Mrs. Small's eyes were filled with tears. She looked at Sasha; both of their faces shared the same anguish. She placed her hands on top of Sasha's.

"Joanne, take your hands off her. I know it's hard, but you have to be strong. We can't have that evil in this house."

Mrs. Small removed her hands from Sasha's. She continuously shook her head while walking away. Sasha remained on her knees, bawling her eyes out. Reverend Small turned his back to her. He closed his eyes and clenched his tattered Bible. I couldn't stand to see her in so much pain. I reached for her hands to help pick her up off the floor.

"Sasha, come on. Let's go."

She batted my hand away. "No! Take your fucking hands off me. Get away from me. I hate you." Sasha stood and sprinted toward the door.

Reverend Small continued to stand with his back turned.

"As hurtful as it is to see my child in pain, I cannot condone homosexuality. God works in mysterious ways. In time, she will learn to understand that your cheating on her was a blessing. It was God's way of showing her that her perverse lifestyle was against His will. It helped to prove that a woman can hurt her just as deeply as a man could. Maybe now, she can see that she was living wrong, repent, and come back to her senses."

I wanted so badly to curse him the fuck out, but I had done enough damage. Being disrespectful to Sasha's parents would only make matters worse. Instead, I held my tongue and rushed out to try to find Sasha again.

I had no clue of where she could be. I called Silka first and then Jaime, hoping she went to them. I gave them the 411 on what happened.

"Come on, Sam. Why would you do that? You love this girl," Silka said.

"Sam, she lost family and friends being with you. What would possess you to fuck Sapphire?" Jaime asked.

"I know, I know. I fucked up. It fucks me up inside that she doesn't know that I appreciate her sacrifices for our love, but I don't need a lecture from you two right now. I need your help."

After getting yelled at by both of them, they agreed to let me know immediately if she contacted them.

After driving around aimlessly looking for her for nearly an hour and a half, I decided to call it quits, go home, and wait to see if she would come back. When I pulled up to my building, I was sure she was home because her car was parked in front. I parked, jumped out of my truck, and ran up the walkway to my building.

I stepped inside the house—all the lights were off. I noticed her shoes by the door, and her keys and purse were on the kitchen table. The next thing I noticed was how eerily quiet it was.

"Sasha? Baby? Are you in here? Baby, I'm sorry. I fucked up, and I was stupid. She didn't mean anything to me."

I didn't hear a response.

I wasn't sure if she was giving me the silent treatment or if she stopped by but left again. I was frustrated. I yelled even louder, hoping she would finally answer me.

"Can you at least say something? You could at least talk to me."

I walked down the hallway where I saw the light shining from my partially closed bedroom door. I figured she was crying to herself in our bedroom. I knocked on the door.

"Baby, are you OK?"

She still didn't say anything.

"All right, enough of this shit. Please, talk to me," I said.

When I pushed open the door, my heart felt like it was going to beat out of my chest. I gasped and screamed. I fell back against my dresser to keep myself from fainting. Fear fluttered in the pit of my stomach. Sasha's lifeless body lay limp across my bed, holding a note and the picture of us enjoying ourselves during Pride Week. The empty prescription bottle that once contained my sleep medication was overturned on my nightstand. I snapped myself out of it and said, "No . . . no . . . no . . . shit! Oh my God, baby, please, wake up. I need you. Please don't die on me!"

I ran over to her and scooped her up in my arms. I wiped my eyes with the back of my hand. She didn't give me a response when I shook her. I tapped her on the face, praying that she was just unconscious and wasn't dead. I rested my head on her chest to see if it would rise and fall and listened for a heartbeat, but it didn't rise, and I heard nothing. I checked the inside of her wrist for a pulse and felt nothing there either. I fumbled with my cell phone; my hands shook as I struggled to dial 911. As soon as the operator picked up, I spoke frantically.

"Nine-one-one. What is your emergency?" the operator asked.

"Oh my God. My partner isn't breathing. She has no pulse, and I think she tried to kill herself by swallowing a lot of my prescription sleeping pills."

"OK, ma'am. Do you have an idea of how long it's been since she took the pills?"

"No . . . I don't know. She's dying. I can't live without her."

"Try to remain calm, ma'am. I need some more information from you, and then I'll send help right away. When you end this call with me, if you know how to perform CPR properly, try your best to administer that until help arrives."

After giving the operator the necessary info, I told her that the door would be open for the EMS workers. As soon as the 911 operator assured me that the paramedics were on their way and should be there any minute, I ended the call. I let the phone fall from my hand and rocked Sasha in my arms, silently praying that the operator put a rush on the ambulance. I repeatedly attempted to give Sasha CPR. I even stuck my fingers down her throat to force her to throw up the pills . . . but nothing.

I felt like her life was slowly slipping away, and there was nothing I could do about it. I wept hysterically.

"Just hold on. The ambulance is on its way. I'm so sorry, baby. Please don't die on me," I said, praying that somehow, she could hear me.

There was a bang on my door. I held Sasha in my arms and rocked. The paramedics and cops rushed in and had to pry Sasha out of my arms. I was too shell-shocked to speak and too scared to let her go out of fear that she had killed herself because of me. I ran my hands through my hair, rubbed my face, and put my head down. I prayed my one relapse didn't cause me to lose the only woman I had ever truly been in love with.

Thirteen

Downward Spiral

The doctor walked out of Sasha's room and into the waiting room with a blank facial expression. I didn't know if he was going to say something that would have me jumping for joy or praying to God for forgiveness. He took a deep breath and said, "I'm sorry, ma'am. Ms. Small didn't make it."

My legs almost gave out on me. Had it not been for Dr. Andrews holding me up, I would've fallen to the floor.

I grasped my chest. My hands shook. I didn't want to believe it. Not too long ago, she was alive. I touched her skin, saw her face, and heard her voice. Now, she was dead.

"No no no! Please, God!"

Silka, Jaime, and Dr. Andrews all tried to console me. I felt weighed down with guilt. I replayed every intimate moment, every conversation, and reminisced on the joyful times and even some of the rough ones. There was still so much I wanted to do with her, so many things I wanted to say and experience with her. I wanted to kiss her again. I wanted to feel her skin against mine and make love to her again. I wanted to tell her that she completed me, made me a better, stronger woman than I had ever been before she came into my life, but I'd never get that chance again. Because of my betrayal, I had lost her forever.

Jaime brought me a cup of water, but I didn't need or want water. What I needed was Sasha, and what I wanted was for her to be alive. It was because of my stupidity that she was gone. Silka rubbed my back while I cried in Dr. Andrews's arms.

"We're here for you, Sam. We love you and will help you through this," Silka whispered to me repeatedly.

I calmed myself down and reached for my cell phone.

"Who are you calling?" Jaime asked.

"I have to tell her parents. They have to know."

"Do you want me to make that call for you?" Dr. Andrews asked.

"If not him, I can call for you," Jaime added.

"No, I have to do this. I caused this. Now I have to be woman enough to face her parents and tell them the effect my mistake had on their daughter."

I blocked my number and called the number back that Josephine had used to call me when Sasha went to her parents' house. Mrs. Small picked up.

"Hello?"

"It's me, Mrs. Small. It's Samantha," I said.

"What do you want? I can't take any more of this. You and that girl of mine are going to put me in an early grave." Her statement broke me down again.

"Mrs. Small . . . She's gone."

"What do you mean 'gone'?"

"She's dead. She killed herself after leaving your house tonight."

Mrs. Small let out a deafening shriek. I heard her wailing uncontrollably before she dropped the phone. Tears cascaded down my face as I waited for her to pick up the phone again. It sounded like she was crying to someone else in the background. I couldn't hear everything said in the conversation, but it sounded like Reverend Small was screaming and crying also.

Someone picked up the phone.

"*You* did this. It's because of *you* that my child is dead. You were a curse on my family. Don't ever call this house again. You've done enough to damn our family," Reverend Small said before ending the call.

I collapsed in defeat. Silka and Dr. Andrews embraced me again. I reached in my pants pocket where I had stuffed the note and picture she had left behind. I needed to see that picture. I wanted to go back to that day. We were happy then. She loved me, and I loved her, and she wasn't stressed about coming out. Most importantly, I wanted to go back to a time where I didn't fuck everything up, and she was still alive. I held the picture tightly. I rocked and wept as I clutched it to my chest. Dr. Andrews continued to hold me. I felt his legitimate concern for me. I patted his arm, and he let me go. I unfolded Sasha's note and took a deep breath.

"What's that?" Dr. Andrews asked.

"Sasha . . . Sasha wrote this before . . ." I started to get choked up again.

"If you're not ready to read it yet, don't force yourself," he said.

"I need to read this now. I want to get it over with. Prolonging it will only fuck me up later."

My hands trembled as I opened the note.

To Sam and my family,

Sam, with you, I experienced what it truly means to love. The times spent together and the memories we've shared made me fall in love with you and showed me the beauty of our relationship. I learned that love is love, regardless if it's straight or gay. My love for you was so great that I sacrificed my family and friends to be with you. When you cheated on me tonight, on top of the pain from my sacrifice, I felt that even though I love you, our relationship would never be the same and I'd end up wounded like you. I didn't want that to happen. You're stronger than I could ever be, and I've always admired that about you. I'm sorry if you felt I wasn't there for you during your nightmares. Sam, you have to let go of the pain from your past and move on. Our lives don't have a rewind, only a forward. You can't dwell on the past because you can't change it. I leave you with this scripture, and I hope this helps you to get better.

"Let all bitterness and wrath and anger and clamor and slander be put away from you, along with all malice. Be kind to one another, tenderhearted, forgiving one another, as God in Christ forgave you." Ephesians 4:31–32

I closed my eyes tightly. The paper rattled in my hands as I tried to force myself to finish the note.

Mom and Dad, I never meant to be an embarrassment or a disappointment. Even though you may feel that I don't know what love is and believe I'm confused, both of you have taught me the definition through the scriptures:

"Love is patient, love is kind. It does not envy, it does not boast, it is not proud. It is not rude, it is not self-seeking, it is not easily angered, it keeps no record of wrongs." 1 Corinthians 13:4–5

I love Samantha, and I couldn't hide who I was anymore. I've tried for years to lock it away and pretend I didn't have an attraction to women, but I couldn't live my life in a lie any longer. Even though I am a sinner, I know God will always love me because He knows my heart.

*While I know God will always love me, the fact that my
entire family turned their backs on me hurt me beyond
measure. Losing my family felt like being left by God. I
can't live without Him, and I can't live without my family.
I know you believe I'm destined to go to hell because of
my lifestyle, but I don't believe that.*

*I leave you with this scripture, and I hope it helps you
to understand that God doesn't hate me:*

*"But in all these things we overwhelmingly conquer
through Him who loved us. For I am convinced that
neither death, nor life, nor angels, nor principalities,
nor things present, nor things to come, nor powers, nor
height, nor depth, nor any other created thing, shall be
able to separate us from the love of God, which is in
Christ Jesus our Lord." Romans 8:37–39*

Tears rolled down my cheeks. I refolded the note and
picture. I put them both in my pocket. I knew the words
Sasha had written were what her parents and I needed,
but right then, all I wanted was to see her again.

A week had passed since Sasha died. Despite showing
Sasha's family her note, they didn't help me organize her
funeral. None of her friends came. The only member of
her family who showed up was her mother. Because
of how Sasha passed, her father wouldn't perform the
service. He even asked other reverends in the area if they
could respect his wishes and decline to perform the service. Dr. Andrews found a friend of his family who was
an ordained minister to do it. Dr. Andrews was a godsend.
He made all of the funeral arrangements. There was no
way I would've been able to make them.

For the most part, I was okay during the memorial service. With my shoulders slumped and my head hung low, I felt myself shake. A chill ran through me. My voice shook as I unfolded the speech I had prepared for Sasha. The words wouldn't come out, and my hands wouldn't stop trembling.

Dr. Andrews stood next to me, placed his hand on my shoulder, and said, "Take your time. Everything you're going to say is coming from the heart, so don't worry about anything else."

I tried my best to be strong when I shared my words for her. The hard part was watching them lower her casket into the ground. That's when I lost all of my strength and wept. My chest heaved with stress and guilt.

Mrs. Small walked up to me. "You should cry. This all happened because of you. My child's blood is on your hands. I hope you rot in hell."

She dabbed her eyes with her tissue and walked away. Her words sent a chill to my bones and made me feel worse. A flood of emotions overwhelmed me. In my mind, I was responsible. If I didn't try to turn her out, her feelings for women would have stayed dormant. She would still have her family, and she would've still been alive. If I hadn't cheated on her—if I were more persistent and sympathetic with helping her cope with losing her family and friends—none of this shit would've happened. The truth is, I felt responsible for her death, and I hated myself because of that.

Four months passed. I was emotional, but my fucking emotions are what got me in this shit. I didn't deserve her; I didn't deserve to mourn. This was all my fault. I fucking did this. My emotions made me push her when she was pulling away. I lived out loud and pressured her to be the same way instead of being patient. My emotions caused me to lose control of my ego and sex drive. I betrayed her trust and everything our love stood for when I fucked Sapphire on the same bed we made love on—our bed. I shouldn't have crossed that line. My emotions didn't let me say the things I needed to and caused me to misspeak out of anger. Had I taken control over my fucking emotions from the jump, Sasha would still be alive. If there were anything I could do to take back everything I did, I would, but I can't, and I have to live with that for the rest of my life.

The only thing I stayed consistent with was my photography business. I went back to smoking cigarettes, hunting and fucking women on the fence, and fucking people for money in the VIP rooms. I stopped going to my rape survivor meetings and seeing Dr. Andrews. I felt numb. I regretted not having the opportunity to tell her I loved her one last time. Her suicide robbed me of that chance and left me feeling as if I had nothing else to live for.

I contemplated suicide, believing that in death, we would be together again. I ran a warm bath for myself, lay in the tub, and broke the razor I used to shave my legs. I pulled the blades out of my broken razor and put them against the top of my wrists. My hands trembled as I pressed the blades into my skin. I bled but stopped myself before I went too deep. I shook my head and cursed myself for not being able to go through with it.

Come on, you fucking pussy. You're so weak and pathetic—you can't even kill yourself.

My nightmares were happening more frequently now and were worse than before. Now, I had dreams of me killing Sasha or seeing visions of her lifeless body on our bed with blood on my hand. I tried to block out those thoughts, focus on other things to think about, but the aftermath of my stupid mistakes haunted me. Seeing her face again in my dreams felt so real. Every time I closed my eyes, I was forced to relive that painfully sad moment when I found Sasha dead on our bed.

Besides my photography business, I spent the rest of my alone time lying low inside my apartment, lounging on the couch doing nothing but chain-smoking cigarettes and drowning myself in alcohol to numb myself from the pain, but neither of those things filled the void in my heart. I felt alone. I felt empty.

I avoided talking to Silka and Jaime. I didn't return their calls or texts even though they both checked on me every day, and if they came over, I didn't answer the door. If they came by the club, I found ways to avoid them. I was on a downward spiral, and I didn't want to bring them down with me.

One morning, Silka, Jaime, and Dr. Andrews surprised me and did an intervention. I was headed to the gym to work out when I opened my door and saw them camped out in the hallway.

"Shit!" I exhaled.

"Why are you avoiding us?" Silka asked.

"I just haven't been in the mood for company," I said.

"Company? I thought we were supposed to be a family," Jaime added.

"We're *not* company. We're your *family,*" Silka said.

"It's nothing personal. I don't want to drag all of you into my personal bullshit."

"Isn't that what Sasha did to you?" Dr. Andrews said.

The mention of her name immediately made me emotional. My eyes began to water as the feeling of guilt washed over me.

"I don't have time for this right now. I have to go," I told them. Jaime and Silka blocked my path.

"Hear us out first. If you don't care about what we have to say, you can go on your way," Dr. Andrews said.

I sighed. "Fine."

We walked into my apartment. I plopped down on the sofa and awaited their rant about me fucking up.

"What's up with you, Sam?" Jaime asked.

"I'm good." I rolled my eyes at her.

"You're *not* good. Since Sasha died, you've been regressing," Dr. Andrews commented.

"Yeah, well . . . The person that I became with her died when she did."

"And this is how you honor her memory? Did you *really* love her?" Dr. Andrews asked.

He was starting to annoy me and fuck with my mind. He knew the answer to that damn question.

"You know I did. I still do," I replied sharply.

"Well, if you do, why are you shitting on her memory by going back to your old habits?" Silka said.

"You don't know what you're talking about," I responded.

"I don't work at the club anymore, but you know I still talk to Cinnamon and some of the other girls. They said you're back to fucking people in the VIP rooms," Jaime said.

"Those bitches need to stop worrying about me and worry about their own money. I'm handling mine." I pulled out my pack of cigarettes.

"You're back to smoking again too? I thought you quit?" Silka asked.

"I'm not a quitter," I said jokingly.

No one laughed but me. I got ready to spark one, but Jaime snatched it from my lips. I flipped her off, and she frowned at me. "Sam, I know you're hurting. I know you're angry, but Sasha gave you the best advice in that letter she left you," Dr. Andrews said.

My hands started shaking.

"How have your dreams been, Sam?" he asked.

I swallowed hard. "Not good," I answered.

"You have friends that love you, but you're pushing them away just like you felt Sasha did to you. You know how you can keep her memory alive? By applying all the positive things, she brought into your life. Most importantly, you have to let go of that anger."

I thought about Sasha's note. I remembered how happy I was with her, but then I thought about the look on her face when she found out I cheated on her. Tears flooded my eyes.

"What I have to do is get you guys away from me. I just want to be left the fuck alone!" I didn't mean those words, but I was angry and didn't want to be called out about my negative behavior.

"All right, Sam," Dr. Andrews said. "Ladies, let's do what she asks. Samantha, I want you to be alone with your thoughts today and think about your actions."

They walked out, and I slammed the door behind them. I poured myself a tall glass of Hennessey and continued to drink my pain away until I passed out on the floor.

I was a little girl again, but I was at the strip club. I was standing there naked. Men were reaching for me. They wanted to fuck me. They cornered me. Hundreds of them surrounded me. As soon as it looked like I was done for, I felt Sasha's arms around me, holding me the way she did when I had my nightmares. I felt her warmth, I felt the love, and I didn't want the feeling to end. Sasha held my face in her hands. She kissed me and told me that she loved me and forgave me.

I woke up crying hysterically. I went to my nightstand and pulled out our pictures and her note and read it over and over again. I did what Dr. Andrews suggested. I reflected on my actions. I thought about my childhood. I thought about the prostitution, being in jail, meeting Cheryl, and all the games I played with countless women. I thought about how happy I was with Sasha and the plans we had for the future like opening the photography studio and one day starting a family. I still wanted those things, but I was scared. I didn't know if I would be able to obtain those things on my own.

Eventually, I prepared myself for work at the club, but I had so much on my mind.

I walked into the dressing room to get ready for my set. Even though I drank a lot that morning, I never felt so sober. I looked around the room at all of the other girls. None of them had dreams or goals of getting out of that place. It happens—we get so used to making fast, easy money that we get comfortable and stay until we're washed up.

"Why are you staring at me like that, bitch? What are you looking at?" Sapphire said.

Her calling me out my name broke my trance.

"Not much," I replied, rolling my eyes.

"Don't tell me you're still pining over that stupid bitch who killed herself over you."

Without warning, I rushed over and punched the shit out of her. Blood poured from her nose. I kicked her in the stomach, dragged her by her hair to the ground, and slammed her head on the floor repeatedly. She balled up in the fetal position, trying her best to protect her face as I continuously kicked and stomped her. Some of the girls ran for help, but no one dared fuck with me while I beat her ass. Jerrod and three bouncers came to pry me off her and break us up. Some of the girls helped to pick up Sapphire off the ground and walked her to the bathroom to get cleaned up.

"What the fuck is the matter with you? She can't go on stage like that," Jerrod said.

"She should've watched her mouth. She said some slick shit about Sasha."

"You see, now *I'm* mad. I'm tired of you fucking with my money, Isis. First, you turn these bitches out and cause them to either quit or get fired. You come in here whenever you fucking want and don't give a shit about keeping a steady flow of customers in here. Now, you're fucking up one of my big moneymakers because your little feelings got touched that she said something about a bitch you dogged out."

I punched Jerrod in the mouth with all my might. The bouncers grabbed me, but he waved them off. Blood dripped from his mouth. He looked me up and down, then gave me a right cross of his own that leveled me. He kicked me in the stomach, then stood over me and glared.

"Bitch, have you lost your fucking mind? Pack your shit. Your ass is outta here. You're not gonna be putting your hands on anybody else in my motherfucking business. You think I can't find some other pretty pussy to take your place? You're not special. There are millions

of girls out there that can shake their ass better than you."
He looked at the bouncers and said, "I pay you niggas to
secure my property, right?"

They nodded.

"Well, escort this piece of shit out of here."

"Fuck you, Jerrod! Fuck you and this place. I hope this
place burns to the fucking ground!"

"Whatever, bitch!"

He looked angrily at his security staff, then pointed at
one of the newer ones and said, "Nigga, what's your job
title here?"

The bouncer stammered, "I'm a bouncer, sir."

"Well, what are you waiting for? Bounce this bitch on
out of here."

All of the bouncers stood there looking stupid, staring
at one another. That only pissed Jerrod off even more.

"Did y'all not hear me? What the fuck did I say? Get
her the fuck out of here. If this bitch isn't out of my sight
in the next minute, all of you niggas are fired along with
her."

I grabbed my bag as one of the bouncers reached for
me.

"Keep your fucking hands off of me! I'm leaving!"

I cleaned out my locker and walked out the door, not
knowing what the future held for me, but I knew it would
be positive because I was getting out of that hellhole.

Fourteen

Dream Come True

I sat home depressed for a few days. I was glad to be free from stripping, but I was afraid of what I would do for the future. I heard someone knock at my door. I wasn't in the mood for company, but I forced myself to get off my ass and look through the peephole to check to see who the hell it was and what they wanted. One of my neighbors stood in front of my door. I rarely talked to her, so I wondered what she could want. I opened the door.

"Hey, girl! I'm sorry I haven't given you these sooner, but I've been staying at my man's house and haven't checked my mail in weeks. The mailman mixed some of your mail with mine."

I looked at the stack she handed me. There was a letter from Chase Bank.

"Thanks," I replied.

"Sorry about that. You should curse his ass out the next time he delivers mail here."

"I probably will. Thanks again."

"No problem, girl. I'll see you later. Oh, before I forget . . . I'm thinking of getting one of those dope portraits you be making. You think you could hook me up?"

At this point, I would have said anything to get rid of her. I wanted to know what the letter said.

"Yeah, I got you. Whenever you're ready, we'll get it done."

"Thanks, girl! I'll be in touch." She headed back to her apartment.

I waved and slowly closed the door. I held the envelope in my hands. I was anxious yet cautious at the same time. While I wanted to know what the letter said, I was scared it was a rejection letter, and then I would be even more depressed. I decided to toughen up and ripped open the letter. I took a deep breath before I started to read it. Tears dripped down my face as I read the first words of the letter: *Congratulations! Your loan has been successfully approved.* I looked up at the ceiling and thanked God. I thanked Sasha, and I thanked God again for placing her in my life.

Reading that good news sparked the motivation I needed to get my life in order. I patched things up with Silka and Jaime. They were my family, and they were happy to have me back. I invited them to my place.

"I'm sorry I've been such a bitch to you guys lately."

"It's okay. We're used to it," Jaime said jokingly.

I punched her playfully.

"We're happy you came to your senses. We've been through everything together. If you're hurting, we're hurting. We're a family. Don't forget that," Silka said.

I cried. I always wanted a family like Sasha's. I wanted that closeness that they had and people to share memories with, but unlike Sasha's family, I wanted one that would love me unconditionally. While Jaime and Silka were not related to me by blood, they had always been there for me. I had what I needed all along.

The next thing I decided to do to get my life in order was to get a new tattoo.

"Are you sure about this?" Jaime asked.

"I'm positive," I smiled.

We went to Whatever Tattoo on St. Marks Place in Manhattan. I dragged Silka and Jaime to join me on my latest spontaneous epiphany.

"Tattoos are kind of . . . permanent. What if you fall in love with another woman?" Silka asked.

"If that happens, she'll have to understand that Sasha will always be in my heart. Besides, it's not that big."

"It's not, but you're still getting her name across your sternum. That shit is going to hurt like hell," Silka said.

"It will, but losing her hurt more than any pain this tattoo can give me. Plus, this way, she will always be a part of me. I can never forget her."

I had my "Pain Is Love" tattoo altered, so it read, "Love is patient, Love is kind." I wanted to get rid of the negative memory that my old tattoo represented.

I made more steps to improve my life by going back to my rape survivor meetings, and I started my therapy sessions with Dr. Andrews again. It took me awhile, but by talking to him about my past and Sasha's death, I slowly started to heal.

I sat in Dr. Andrews's office. He stood in front of his bookcase, looking at one of his old college photos. As always, I waited to hear his words of wisdom.

"When I went to Howard University, I was a part of Alpha Phi Alpha. My roommate and frat brother, Ron, who I'm still good friends with today, used to have a quote for everything. He was one of the first people I ever confided in about being raped as a child. When I told him how it had bothered me all my life, Ron gave me this quote by Wayne Dyer: 'If you change the way you look at things, the things you look at change.'

"Ron helped me to see that even though being raped was a horrible and life-altering experience, I wouldn't be who I am today if I never went through that trauma. He told me that I was stronger than most people because I knew how to live through adversity. Hearing those words helped me to realize it myself.

"That quote Ron gave me helped me to see things differently."

"How can I turn anything positive out of my fucked-up life?" I asked.

"Despite doing time, you have your own small business, a humongous apartment, and through all the hard times you've faced, you have friends who care about you. Above all, you're alive, healthy, and moving forward. You always have to look at those things as blessings."

There were times when I would have terrifying nightmares, but Dr. Andrews told me to think of Sasha and how she used to hold me lovingly after them. That memory soothed me, and I was somewhat able to tame the nightmares.

I visited my old strip club one last time after hearing they had a new bad-ass stripper named Tisha, The Chocolate Goddess. The line to get in the club was wrapped around the block. After waiting awhile, I went in.

"What the fuck are you doing here, Isis?"

"I come in peace. I just want to check out the show."

"Yeah, I bet. Look, I'm not trying to have you bring any drama in my club tonight."

"I promise I won't start any shit."

"If I see the slightest hint of you fucking with my girls, you're out of here."

"Understood."

I watched Tisha do her thing on stage. The club was packed, and the speakers pulsated with Vanity's "Nasty Girl" bumping from the speakers. I looked around the club and hardly recognized anyone. There were mostly new faces.

The lights dimmed, and the DJ announced the club's latest attraction, Tisha.

She was exactly as her name described, a chocolate goddess. She had smooth, blemish-free chocolate skin and a full-figured shape that rivaled mine. She was tall, about my height, five foot eight, but the three-inch heels that she wore made her look even taller. She walked the stage with such swagger, as if all of the men with their lustful leers were beneath her. I loved her confidence, and I remembered how I used to feel that way . . . so invincible and powerful. I heard all the oohs and aahs from the crowd. Money flooded the stage, and I'll admit, I was a little jealous. She was masterful on the pole, doing tricks I would have never even attempted and doubted I could ever do.

Seeing her up there on that stage, killing it, reminded me of when the crowd used to go crazy and fawn over me like that. I was a little angry too that Jerrod had so easily and quickly found a successor to me for the club, but the show needed to go on, I guess.

I knew firsthand that eventually, this lifestyle loses its luster, and I hoped Tisha, "The Chocolate Goddess," was smart enough to have a plan B after things started to go sour.

A few months later, I read in the newspaper that there was a huge raid on my old strip club after numerous reports that it was a cover-up for a prostitution ring. Right next to the article was a picture of Sapphire and Jerrod in handcuffs, both crying. I was blessed to have gotten out when I did.

Another step I took toward improving was opening a legitimate studio. With the loan, the money I earned from Virginia, my photography, and working in the club, I had more than enough money to get my studio started. Silka backed me as a cosigner, and Jaime helped with searching for good locations for the business. Five months later, I opened S&S Studios (Sasha and Samantha's).

"Wow, Sam! You really did it! Sasha would be so happy for you," Dr. Andrews said.

"Thanks. I would've never accomplished this if it weren't for her. I wish she were here to see this."

"She *is* here." Jaime pointed to the massive picture in the entranceway of the studio.

Before the grand opening, I looked through all of the photos I had taken of Sasha. I found a great picture of her wearing a sexy business suit. I had the picture blown up and displayed it in the entrance of the studio with the words "*In loving memory of Sasha Small*" printed underneath it.

At the grand opening—even though I sent numerous invitations—I never expected any of Sasha's family to come. So, I was shocked when I saw Mrs. Small standing in front of the portrait of Sasha. I didn't want to approach her because I didn't know if she still held animosity toward me.

She turned around in tears. Our eyes connected. I took a deep breath and approached her. She met me halfway. She took me into her arms and affectionately embraced me. I was surprised at first, but I welcomed our brief hug. Once she let me go, Mrs. Small left the studio. I knew she would never understand the feelings Sasha and I shared, but in that hug, I felt she knew I loved Sasha, and the love we shared was real. I never saw Mrs. Small again after that day, but I would never forget it. I felt at peace.

With the studio opening, business tripled. I hired a competent staff, and Jaime worked there on weekends to help out.

My life was slowly coming together, but I still felt something was missing. What I wanted would be life changing. I wanted it more than anything and feared it at the same time. It was unfortunate that I needed a man's help for it, but if there was one man I trusted, it was Dr. Andrews. It took a lot of begging and pleading for my case with him, but he finally gave in.

He agreed to be a sperm donor, so I could have a child through artificial insemination. We agreed he would sign over his parental rights but would be involved in the child's life. I didn't want anything monetarily from him. I would take care of this child on my own.

I had planned to do this with Sasha, but now, I was doing this *for* Sasha. Having this child would help me to correct all the bullshit that happened in my life because I would do everything in my power to make my child's life phenomenal. I made very good money with my business, so financially, I was stable. Most importantly, I knew I was ready mentally and emotionally.

Dr. Andrews and I went to American Fertility in Manhattan. They were very accepting of me being gay, and my request to raise my child on my own. On the first try, my dream of having a child was fulfilled. During the process in week ten, I got a surprise.

"Ms. Miller, you're having twins," the doctor told me.

"No fucking way! What did you say? I'm having *twins?*" I said excitedly.

"Yes! Congratulations," he said.

Dr. Andrews, Dom, Silka, and Jaime hugged me. I felt as if Sasha's presence were in the room. I felt her smiling down on me.

In week twenty, I found out the sexes. They turned out to be fraternal twins, a girl and a boy.

"Well, this is a good thing. Your daughter will have a brother to look after her," Jaime said.

"She won't need him for that because she'll have me. I'll be enough protection for both of them," I said.

"Have you thought of names?" Dr. Andrews asked.

I already knew what my children's names would be the moment I heard I was having fraternal twins. I would name my daughter the same name tattooed on my chest—the same name of the mother they would've had if she were still alive, and the same name of the woman who would forever be my first life partner—Sasha. I decided to name my son after me—Samuel. I would prepare him to be a real man—a better man than my father was.

The most important thing about having a son was I knew the love that I had for him would truly end my hatred for men. I had gotten better, thanks to Dr. Andrews and Dom, but loving my son would free me from the bonds of hatred for good.

Two years passed. Jaime met a man named Charles and was engaged. Silka and Dom were expecting their second child, a son who they planned to name after Dominic. I had been happy raising my two kids. My business was still flourishing, but not a day had gone by that I didn't think of Sasha. It's because of those thoughts that every year on her birthday, I took the children to her grave.

My kids will know who she was. They will know the woman who taught me how to love.

I placed two dozen roses on her gravestone; then I faced Dr. Andrews.

"I'm going to talk to her now. Can you give me a minute?"

"I'll take the kids. Take as long as you need," he said as he patted me on the back and began walking away to give me space.

I nodded. Through everything, Dr. Andrews had been a great friend. I never thought I would ever consider a man a friend, but I owed a lot to him. He never betrayed my trust, and he felt like the father I never had.

"Dr. Andrews?"

"Yes, Sam?"

"Thank you . . . for everything."

"It was my pleasure," he smiled.

For the next half hour, I knelt, closed my eyes, and spoke as if Sasha's spirit were listening. I knew she was there. I felt her spirit. I always began with an apology before going into the current happenings in my life. When I finished, I stood up and stared at the sky. The sun was shining on me. There's an old saying that time heals all wounds. I still think that saying is bullshit. It wasn't time that healed my wounds—it was love.

The End